5.00

THE GIRL IN THE MANOR

A.J. RIVERS

PROLOGUE

Mary noticed the man as soon as he walked into the bus station. There was something about him that didn't look like he fit in with the rest of the people milling around the cavernous open space. She couldn't put her finger on what it was. The passengers, families, and friends gathering at the different gates, waiting in the rows of metal chairs, and moving in and out of the bank of glass doors along the front of the building covered a full range of people. Like a microcosm of the city around them. Suits and sleek satchels, jeans and baggy t-shirts, grungy backpacks sitting beside expensive matching luggage. All kinds of passengers took advantage of the fleet of buses that traveled from the city hub. He didn't stand out against them.

Yet, she couldn't take her eyes off him. There was something about him. Something that wouldn't let go of her attention. But Mary didn't know if that was a good thing or a bad one. She watched him walk into the station and waited for him to glance around in that way most people do when they come into a crowded space like the station. Even when they know where they are and where they are going, most people take a few seconds to evaluate their surroundings. But not this man. He walked in and kept his eyes locked directly ahead of him. He didn't even seem to notice the people moving around him as he crossed the high shine-polished linoleum floor. Rather than him navigating around people and finding his path, the crowd parted for him and his determined stride.

He wasn't carrying any luggage. Not even a small bag over his shoulder. He wore tailored charcoal pants and a white button-up tucked in and rolled to his elbows. The belt and matching shoes looked expensive, even from the distance. But she couldn't decipher the look on his face. It was intense and stiff, but that wasn't all that different from many of the other people rushing to get to the next bus or juggling little children traveling with them. This is the part of travel that rarely creates relaxed, happy people. This man looked driven to get through the room, focused directly ahead of him. Mary watched him until he disappeared around a corner. Part of her wanted to follow him, but she stopped herself. That would be letting her curiosity go too far.

She pulled out her phone and turned on the camera to record the room around her.

"Here it is, folks. The majestic bus station. Perhaps not the most elegant of transportation, but we'll say I'm doing something good for the environment by joining up with the masses for the trip rather than driving myself. We'll just keep that it's super cheap as a secret between us."

Mary turned the camera to herself and smiled into it before turning off the screen. It was the fourth snippet of video she had made since the morning before, when she woke up with the urge to go on a trip. Her tripod made it possible to record her packing her bags while she talked to her audience about not knowing where she was going to end up. Another clip followed her as she drove to the bus station, and her third accompanied her as she walked through the parking lot and inside. She still hadn't decided where she would end up or how long she was going to stay. The income she was building up from her vlogs would fund whatever adventure she ended up on, but it had to be something worth watching.

She made her way closer to the board announcing the departures and scanned the various options for where to go. The calendar had just barely ticked over to September, and the weather wasn't yet cool enough to really justify an escape to Florida. Mary also didn't think she could bear that many hours on a bus. Her family made that road trip once when she was younger, and that had been challenging enough. Stuffing herself into a carpet seat and being cozy with a stranger for several hours longer than that old school road trip wasn't appealing. New York was too much of a cliché. The beach didn't seem far enough away. She finally settled on Baltimore, figuring she could get good footage out of touring the harbor and opened her phone to buy her ticket.

Done with the purchase, Mary headed for the information desk to get a luggage tag for her bag. This was only the third trip she chronicled for her channel, but she wanted to keep up the tradition of getting a luggage tag each time. Maybe she would turn them into a scrapbook. Or maybe they would all end up in the bottom drawer of her nightstand. Either way, she was going to continue on.

She dug through her bag in search of lip balm as she stepped into the line. She took out her phone and held it up as she waited for the person in front of her to finish.

"On my way to Baltimore!" she said. "It's been years since I've been there, and I'm sure I'll find a lot of new things. I actually don't remember anything from my last trip except for my sister singing that song from *Hairspray* about twelve times during the day. And maybe the aquarium. I think that was Baltimore. Well, we'll find out. It's only about a three-hour ride, so I'll be there in plenty of time to find a hotel and get some exploring in today. What do you think I should have for dinner? Hmmm..."

The person in front of her finished talking, and she turned to the desk. It wasn't until she turned away with several luggage tags in her hand that she realized she had been standing right behind the man she watched walk into the station. He disappeared into the back of the station again, and Mary went to the chairs to wait the hour until her bus left.

Her wait would last less than five minutes.

The impossibly bright blast tore through the station, screams faint behind the aftermath of the deafening sound. Shards of fractured linoleum and hot metal rained down on Mary, where she sprawled on the floor. Beneath her, pinned against what remained of the broken floor, her phone continued to record. It drew in the chaos, chronicling the screams. Her body blocked it from the smoke and flames, but the sounds of terror wore on in the darkness.

CHAPTER ONE

THREE YEARS AGO

The ground swirled beneath her as she looked over the edge of the tower. It was so far down. Further than she thought when she first scrambled out the window and onto the narrow ledge. She dropped down to the stone floor, pulling her knees up to her chest. The cold of the stones soaked through the thin fabric of her dress on her back and into the bones of her spine. It protruded from her skin, raising up in defined ridges like a prehistoric creature preserved in mud. Her body was worn as thin as the dress she'd been wearing for the last six months.

Breath rattled in her lungs. Her insides might have turned to stone as cold as the tower behind her. But when she leaned her forehead down to her knees and parted her dry, cracked lips to let out her breath, it felt warm on her face. She wrapped her arms tightly around her head to create a dark hollow where her eyes could hide. She breathed again. The warmth was proof she was still alive. No matter what they did. No matter how hard they tried. She was still alive.

But that wouldn't last for long if she didn't move. She didn't have much time until they realized she wasn't in the tiny room where they left her. As soon as the smell of bleach wasn't strong enough, or one called out for her and she didn't immediately appear in front of them, they would discover she was gone. The memory of their voices slid down her back between the ripples of her spine and the cold tower wall.

Sister Abigail. Sister Abigail. Sister Abigail.

She wanted to peel that name away, to scrub it from her skin, to excise it from her being. They inflicted it on her. They crafted her into its image. It brought her to her feet and standing on the ledge again. The ground didn't seem so far now. Just a breath. That's all it would take to reach it.

Her body trembled when she took the step onto the top of the low wall. She didn't know if it was from three days of not eating or simply fear. It could be adrenaline coursing through her, refilling what was systematically emptied. She was trying to shed the shell they built up around her to stifle the being she was when she'd first stepped into the sprawling building attached to The Tower. Wind blew up around her. The cold bit into her skin and threatened to force her down from the edge. It wanted her back in The Tower. It wanted her to behave.

She remembered the heat of her breath against her face, caught in the space of her arms and legs, swirling across her skin as she released it. In those breaths, she had power over the wind. She could take the frigid air into her lungs and release it as warmth. Without another thought, she closed her eyes, wriggled her toes until they hung over the edge of the wall, and jumped.

The air held her for a brief second. In that moment, it felt like she almost flew. Then she plummeted, the ground reaching up to claim her. She could have just released herself into it. It would have been so easy to just let that be the last moment, to finally take herself away from The Tower and the people in it. A voice inside her said it would be vindication. She couldn't be their tool anymore. If she let the ground take her, they would have nothing left to use.

But another voice took over. She would no longer be their tool, but she would have been turned into a weapon against herself. This would only be handing to them now what they would have done to her soon enough. Her usefulness was dissipating. It wouldn't be long until there was nothing left of her that they wanted, and they would give her over to the ground anyway. Her choice was to rob them of what remained of her or to give herself the chance for more.

The choice was made before she heard the voice.

Sister Abigail. Sister Abigail. Sister Abigail.

It called above her, sliding from chilling calm to inciting fury. She was expected to respond the instant she heard the name. Even though it wasn't hers. Even when her body was too weak to hold her up. Even when her voice turned to powder. This time she wouldn't respond. She didn't pull herself up and take the painful steps toward the sound of the voice. She dropped to the ground and dragged herself to the nearest hedge. She didn't call out to them, so they knew she heard them. She whispered to herself, to the ground, to the bushes, to the wind, to the reality beyond the walls, that she was done.

Coarse branches tugged at her dress and cut down to her skin, but it meant something different to her now. The pain didn't push her down. Each puncture and scratch gave her back a piece of herself. That pain was hers. Her body was hers again.

She pressed deeper into the hedges when she heard the voices coming louder. They were out of The Tower now. Heavy black boots were only a few feet ahead of her, but none of the men noticed her. Blond hair tinted dark in places with dried blood became part of the branches. They kept calling out for her. But it was a name she would never respond to again.

Sister Abigail. Sister Abigail. Sister Abigail.

It wasn't her name when she walked into The Tower, and it wasn't her name as she clawed her fingers into the soft dirt to pull the rest of her body beneath the hedges. She had no name. Her own was stripped from her in the two years she spent behind the walls. It was still waiting for her on the other side of them. When she got beyond the stone, beyond the darkness, she could have it back.

Tiny sharp shards of stone and earth filled under her fingernails as she dragged herself closer to the wall. She stared at it every day from the window of The Tower. Every chance she had to hesitate and stare out over the grounds, she looked at the wall. It surrounded the grounds, a bigger, more oppressive version of the barrier of the tower ledge. No one on the outside saw it that way. They didn't know what it held.

The voices behind her were getting louder as the last remnants of sunlight disappeared. Long shadows stretched across the grass and deepened beneath trees and around the smaller buildings scattered among them. It was her chance. She pulled herself out of the row of bushes surrounding the main tower and up to her feet. Her legs shook, but she didn't stop. There was no option left now. She wouldn't let them bring her back. She would make it to the wall and the bars of the iron gate she knew her bones would fit between, or the last thing she would ever feel would be the grass.

The voices were gone, but she knew they weren't. The men had only gone back into The Tower. Any second now, they would turn on the light, a bright beam that swept across the grounds and dissolved away every shadow. She'd have nowhere to hide and nothing to protect her.

The cobblestone path leading from the gate wound to the side, looping in a wide arc to keep it far from The Tower. Anyone following it would first get to a gatehouse. If they got beyond the first, there was another. Beyond that, the path led closer until it finally reached a garage far out of view. Where no one would see people getting out of the car. Where no one would find the car even if they were searching for it.

She stayed off the path until the grass gave way to the cement edge around the stones. The beam of light burst around her, casting her own shadow across the path. It stretched away from her like it was going to separate and try to get to the gate before her body. At least then, part of her would get beyond the grounds. They were coming for her. She couldn't hear them, but she could feel them. Their eyes on her back were like hot pokers.

Her hands hit the cold metal of the gate. She turned her body to press it between the bars. There were people beyond The Tower. She didn't know who they were or where, but she knew they were there. If she could find them, she had a chance.

Her fingers wrapped tightly around the bar in front of her. And her body trembling, barely keeping overwhelming shakes of terror and emotion in check, she wedged herself through. The metal pressed against her, exposing more of her skin to the cold night air. Finally she pushed through, and her body cracked against the sidewalk. She scrambled to her feet again and ran until the adrenaline was gone, and she collapsed to the cold cement of a dark, dirty alley. She didn't care. She rolled to her back and stared up at the stars.

She had her name again.

CHAPTER TWO

NOW

The necklaces are almost identical. They're as close to being exactly the same as the variations in the colors swirling through the pendants allows them to be. I've been sitting on the couch staring down at the necklaces, one rested in each palm, for almost an hour. Bellamy mailed them to me a few days after the second one came from Feathered Nest, but I'm no closer to understanding them now than I was six weeks ago. They mean nothing to me. No matter how often I take them out of the bubble mailer she sent them in or how long I stare at them, I haven't come up with anything else. There are no memories attached to them. Nothing comes up when I look at them or flip them back and forth in my palms.

I don't look up when the front door opens. Sam comes in with a bulging brown paper bag in one hand and a cupholder in the other. He kicks the door closed behind him and carries everything over to me.

"I thought we agreed," he sighs, setting the bag and holder down on the coffee table.

"We agreed I wouldn't obsess over them all day," I point out. "I still have hours ahead of me before I've done that."

"Emma. You need to put them away," he tells me, coming around the table to sit beside me. "It's not doing you any good to spend so much time staring at them. Besides, you're supposed to be on a break."

I lower my hands and let out a sigh. "I know. I just can't stop thinking about these."

My leave of absence from work was supposed to be about giving me time to relax after the last two cases. My supervisor, Creagan, gave me his blessing and told me to take all the time I need. Of course, he's told me that before. He thought I was taking vacation two months ago, when I ended up back in my hometown of Sherwood after the sheriff called to ask for my help. To say he was less than pleased to find out I wasn't sprawled on a plastic lounge chair at a Florida water-park and instead was hunting a serial kidnapper is an understatement. The therapist he compelled me to start visiting after the case I handled earlier this year took his side. But that means they were both supportive when I let them know I'd been staying in Sherwood for a while.

Seven years passed since the last time I was in Sherwood to when I arrived to help investigate the kidnappings. Seven years since I said goodbye to the man I knew I'd give away my future to be with if I didn't tear myself away when I did.

I stayed to work through everything I left behind. Which includes Sheriff Sam Johnson sitting beside me on the couch of what was my grandparent's home. Rediscovering him has been like settling into the house again. They are both so familiar, steeped in memories of when I was younger, and at the same time, different. Sometimes those differences are easier to deal with than what is familiar. They don't bring up the pain. Other times, seeing the change takes my breath away.

In my mind, everything had stayed the same. I walked away from Sherwood and into a different life, locking that one in place. When I put it behind me, everything stopped, and I didn't think about any of the ways it might no longer be the same. Everything that is just as it was when I saw it through the sheen of tears that last day feels like I didn't leave. I can look into Sam's eyes and not see the years. I can walk through the house and see my grandparents' home. It's when I have to face the changes that I remember.

Seeing the slight streaks of silver already appearing around the edges of Sam's hair still makes me pause. His father had streaks like that in his hair when we were children. He was a young man then, just like Sam is now. But age started to creep into his hair when he was barely thirty. The first time I ran my fingers back through Sam's hair and discovered those shimmering strands, it made my breath catch. That was a change I wasn't ready to see. I know the time has passed for him, too. I haven't totally convinced myself I put Sherwood into some sort of time-locked snow globe that stopped everyone within it from changing or aging. But seeing it makes me really face all those years that separate us.

It isn't just seven years since I said goodbye to Sam and walked away without planning to ever come back. It's seven years of days that went by without hearing his voice or finding a note he left me. It's seven years of nights without good night wishes. Seven years of missed birthdays, fireworks, and Christmas trees. Seven years of laughs forming little lines by his eyes and tears we weren't there to help each other through. When I look at him and see the changes, it hits me just how much I've really missed.

I moved on into a life I believed was the right one for me but didn't let myself think about the one he would live after that moment. Now I have to, and it's harder than I could have expected.

Even harder than just facing it is the reality that I still don't know what this means. We haven't talked about it. I don't know if we will. I'm here in Sherwood for my leave of absence, but I don't know how long that will last or what will happen when it's over. My career and the life I built is still back there. Back in the house I inherited from my father. Back with the friends who have seen me through the last seven years. Back with the career I devoted my life to at the expense of everything else.

At some point, I'm going to have to stand at that line and decide what I'm going to do next.

Eating through the elaborate assortment of Chinese food Sam

pulled from the paper bag lets me take my mind off the necklaces and listen to him tell me about his day.

"I've told her at least twenty times if she doesn't want the cat to keep getting up onto the roof of her garage and getting stuck there, she should move the ladder, so it won't climb up it. But she insists Mr. Fluffy will learn to come down the ladder one day, and she will have enriched his life," he's saying.

I shake my head as I reach for another egg roll.

"Maybe she shouldn't have given him a name like Mr. Fluffy. If that was my name, I might try to isolate myself on the roof of a garage, too," I shrug through a mouthful of rice. "But she was about a hundred years old when I was six, so maybe I'm missing some sort of generational significance." Sam laughs as he licks a drip of brown sauce away from his finger. "What?"

"Nothing. You're just so serious about things sometimes," he says.

I shrug. "Happens. Consequence of my line of work."

He slides over and touches a kiss to the side of my head. "Which is why you're here. Taking a break."

I can't help but smile; then something pops into my head. "Speaking of which, are you still up for game night at Janet and Paul's tomorrow?"

He nods. "Absolutely. I'm voting for Clue."

I roll my eyes and stab at a piece of broccoli in the nearest container.

"I'm terrible at Clue."

"Exactly. No game night is as much fun as watching someone who hunts serial killers not be able to figure out which of six fake people killed another fake person in an oddly square mansion," he teases.

I poke the broccoli at him. "Just keep it up. One of these days, they're going to choose Twister, and I'm going to dominate."

He looks like he's going to say something, but his eyes flicker over to the TV. I forgot I had it on. It's been on mute since a particularly annoying commercial played for the third time during the show I was watching while waiting for him. Getting sucked into staring at the necklaces made me forget it was even on. Now the newscaster on the screen stares ahead with a cold, stern look on her face, and a bright red banner across the bottom announces, 'BREAKING NEWS'.

"What's going on?" I ask.

He shakes his head and reaches for the remote to turn the volume back on. "I don't know. But it looks serious."

"...twelve deaths and at least sixty life-threatening injuries have been reported. This number is expected to continue to rise as the dozens brought to local hospitals are examined. Responders have put out emergency calls for assistance to search for anyone who may still be trapped in the destruction. We'll update with further developments as they come in."

Footage from a destroyed building fills the screen along with an information bar.

"The bus station in Richmond," I murmur.

"Why would someone bomb a bus station?" Sam asks.

I shake my head. "I don't know."

But a churning feeling in my gut tightens to a burning knot as I watch workers crawl through the crumbled concrete and shattered glass. Issues with the media and conflicts of interest made the courts issue a change of venue for Jake Logan's trial. I'll be in Richmond for a hearing in two weeks.

CHAPTER THREE

HIM

He never thought he would find her there. When she wasn't in Florida for her vacation and hadn't returned to the house, he didn't know where to look for her. Of all the places he thought of to look for her, this didn't even cross his mind. Perhaps it should have. In a way, it was so obvious. And at the same time, it was the farthest thing from his mind. She wouldn't go back. She hadn't in the years since she left. Not back there, not back to Sherwood.

Of course, that was before he started looking for her.

He knew she left only because of where she ended up. It was different when she first went to college. Younger than the other students and with a completely different educational history because of her tutors and bouncing from school to school as she grew up, Emma didn't immediately fit in. Not that she wanted to melt into the campus and be like the rest of the students. There were far more important things on her mind. She had changed by then. Gone was the wistful, always longing look in her eyes that held all the art she wanted to create. Those eyes once brimmed with paintings and sketches waiting to be committed to paper. The very hum of her breath and the beat of her heart was music. Her lithe body danced with every movement.

But the art that crafted her was gone by the time she stepped into her first college class. That part of her died along with her mother. There was always a feeling that life was designed for her. From the moment of her birth, her future was chosen. She was given freedom. She was told to be who she was and discover what she loved. But there was always the sense she was being prepared for something. It was impossible not to. The fight was in her blood.

It took not knowing what happened that night, when she sat on the stairs and watched her mother wheeled out of the house beneath a white sheet, to push her onto the path toward this future. A future that didn't fit in Sherwood. He knew that feeling. He didn't fit there anymore, either. She didn't know he watched her that night. She didn't know how he tried to take away all the obstacles in her life.

In a way, he knew what it felt like for her to come back. Sherwood had once been a comfortable place, a place where they were welcome, where they fit. But not anymore. Not for either of them. He thought she'd never go back there. She didn't interfere with the house there. She didn't go back for her high school reunion or for the weddings, babies, funerals, and gatherings that marked life marching on for those who stayed within the town.

She never went back for the man who knew her maybe too well.

He missed so much. Years of not being able to be near her, no matter how much he wanted to. Things changed too much. It became too dangerous. All because of that one night. The night he waited for, planned for, readied himself for. It went wrong, and she slipped through his fingers.

Not again. He wouldn't let it happen again. That's why he had to be careful. He had to bide his time and be patient. Everything had to be perfect this time. It all had to fall into place just right. Then he could return and have what was his.

Her being back in Sherwood made it that much harder. Even stepping foot into Sherwood was risky. It was her face on the TV screen that told him where she was. Sitting in the tiny, dark room of a hotel that didn't ask for his identification, he turned on the news and saw her standing beside that face from the past. She got herself entangled in another case and unraveled it in a way no one else could.

He was proud of her. But he couldn't get near her. Not in Sherwood. He'd wait. He'd give her time to tie up the loose ends and then go back home. Home to the house bought so she could go to school. That's where she was when he was finally able to look for her, and that's where he would wait for her to return.

But she didn't. She didn't come back, and he couldn't wait any longer. Too many years kept him away from her before, and he didn't want that to happen again. He had to protect her. He was the only one who could. She might not understand why he did the things he did, but one day she would. One day it would all be so clear to her.

He could only be in town for short bits of time and had to stay away from as many people as he could. Someone might see his face and know who he was. They would reach back into their memories, and find his features, find eyes that had looked at them before. That couldn't happen. He couldn't let even a single person recognize him. Or think they did. If they did, they might mention it to Emma. It would be too much for her. She didn't know. She never knew.

He didn't think he would have to wait for long. She should have finished what she was doing with the case and returned to the house where her life was waiting for her. But she didn't. She stayed and stayed. There were no hearings to draw her back. Not even the police assigned to watch her house made her come back. They were still there. Still taking turns rotating through positions to wait for something to happen. None of them knew what they were waiting for.

He couldn't stay away any longer. He needed to see her, to make sure she was alright. He felt so guilty for all the time they were apart, and for not being able to be with her now. Someday he hoped she would understand. She would know everything he had to go through. All he did to build the life she would one day get to have. It would be worth it then.

That's when he went to Sherwood. He stayed in a hotel far outside of town and drove a car that didn't stand out. He dressed in nondescript clothes and wore a hat or sunglasses. It afforded him the brief visits into town to catch glimpses of her and find out why she was still there. He walked along the sidewalk at dawn and drove the street in the twilight. Something had to be done. Something had to draw her away. There was too much at risk with her here.

CHAPTER FOUR

I'm fairly certain part of taking a leave of absence from work is supposed to be about getting extra sleep and staying in my pajamas for a good portion of the day. There have been a few days when I've happily taken up the offer of staying in my pajamas, but stretching out the hours of sleep just hasn't kicked in. No matter how much I will myself to linger in the covers, my eyes are open before first light, and there's nothing I can do to convince myself to keep sleeping. This morning I had my head buried under the pillow for almost an hour before I finally gave up. There's really no point in trying.

Waking up early is just part of me. Instilled in me when I was young, it only became more important in college and then in training for the Bureau. Becoming an agent is extremely challenging for anyone. A woman just barely at the minimum age to take on the position is at a disadvantage in more ways than one. Slicing off hours of sleep and reallocating that time to working out and studying got me to where I am.

Which currently is standing at the living room window, gripping a mug of coffee and watching the rest of the street try to wake up. There are a few others who catch the first moments of the day like I do. Vanessa, at the end of the street, is a baker and drives away from her little red house, and the husband and three children sleeping inside well before the sun comes up. Two of the elderly neighbors down the other side of the street often greet the sunlight gardening or sitting out on their porch like they can't stand the thought of missing even a single second of the day.

Then there's the jogger. At least, that's how I think of him. He doesn't really jog. It's more of a stroll, his hands stuffed in his pockets and the hood of a sweatshirt pulled up over his head. It's only a few days into September, and the last couple of weeks have seen the temperatures in the early mornings dip low enough to justify the hood. But it's still strange. He walks by every morning and disappears around the corner at the end of the street. I don't recognize him, and he never pauses to wave when he does see one of the neighbors who happens to be up at the ridiculous hour.

It's raining this morning, so I don't expect to see him. Chilly raindrops running down the back of your neck is not the most invigorating way to start the day. Just looking at the gray sky strangling what little bits of sunlight are trying to shine and listening to the droplets falling to the grass makes me want to curl up in a quilt on the couch and not move for a while. Today would be the perfect day to marathon old movies. Since coming here and going back to sleeping in a bed, I haven't been lulling myself to sleep with the familiar favorites. It would be nice to have a visit with them.

But that's going to have to wait. Rain or not, today is booked. Starting with getting the dough put together for the cinnamon rolls I promised for today's game night across the street. I have some errands to run today, so I'll make the dough and let it go through its first proof, form the rolls, and put them in the refrigerator to rise while I'm out. That way I can bake them, and they'll be hot and gooey by the time Sam comes. Baking has never been my strongest suit, but my grandmother taught me these rolls when I was little. I haven't made them in years, but when I got back here, it's like the recipe was still waiting for me. It sank back in, and I've made them three times since my leave of absence began. Not fantastic for any efforts toward healthy eating. Amazing for making my house smell like fall is settling in.

My house. That phrase has started slipping into my vocabulary more and more recently. It used to only apply to the house my father signed over to me when he disappeared. This house is my grandparents' house or the house in Sherwood. When the years built up to separate me from the last time I was here, and I almost never mentioned it to anyone, it became 'the rental house'. But the longer I'm here, the more often it comes to mind as being mine. I like the comfortable, nostalgic feeling that brings. At the same time, it makes it even harder to think about what's going to happen when my break comes to an end. When I go back to my own life, what will this house become?

I down the last of the cup of coffee and make my way into the kitchen to make another and start the rolls. The sky doesn't look like it, but the morning is wearing on. I have a small pot of milk warming on the stove as I line up the rest of the ingredients on the table. Everything is there but the yeast. I dig through the cabinets and search the shelves in the pantry. I know I bought yeast yesterday when I went to the grocery store. It's not something I keep around just for the hell of it, so I had to make a point of buying it to make the rolls for the game today.

The strip of packets isn't sitting in the spice cabinet where I thought it was. It's not in the pantry where the rest of the baking ingredients are kept. I dig through a few of the drawers, but I can't find it. Fractured thoughts suddenly crash into my brain. The necklaces sitting in the living room. A birthday note stuffed down in the cushions of my couch. Mail neatly stacked on my bed. Broken glass scattered on the backseat of a worn-down loaner meant to fit in with a false version of me.

Pressing my hands to the edge of the counter, I squeeze my eyes closed and let out a breath to force the thoughts away. It's just yeast. Just packets of yeast I can't find. Because I put them somewhere other than where I thought I did. Not because someone moved them. I draw in another breath and let it out. Moments like this aren't frequent. But when they hit me, they knock me back. My therapist's phone number sits in my phone, waiting for me to call in this type of situation. But I don't. My leave of absence from work includes a leave of absence from letting her dig around in my life.

The yeast must have fallen out of the grocery bag in the car. The thought hits me, breaking me out of the murky memories, and I head outside, grabbing my keys from the hook by the door on the way out. Lessening down to a mist, the rain isn't as chilling as it would have been a few minutes ago. As soon as the trunk pops open, I see the packages of yeast up against the back. They must have toppled out of a bag when it fell over as I unloaded them yesterday. I grab the packets and am closing the trunk when I notice movement out of the corner of my eye. A dark figure at the corner of my neighbor's yard picks something up off the ground. It takes a second for me to realize it's the man who strolls by in the earliest moments of the morning. The jogger.

I've never seen him out this long after his usual walk. He straightens and slips his hand back into his pocket. I don't see what he picked up, but he keeps his hand tucked there, a fist wrapped around whatever it was. As if he suddenly realizes I'm watching him, he turns his head. It's only for a second, but the face makes my breath catch in my throat. I take a step toward him, trying to make myself breathe, wanting to run toward him, but he looks away again. Without even an acknowledgement, he ducks his head down and continues down the sidewalk.

I stare after him, waiting for him to turn back. Maybe he didn't recognize me. It's been ten years. There's a chance he doesn't know it's me. He could think I'm just someone renting the house.

But why would he be here? He'd have no reason to come if he didn't know I was here. It couldn't have been him. It's just the mist and the memories playing tricks on me.

Suddenly I remember the milk sitting on the stove. Pushing the trunk lid down, I rush back inside. The milk's bubbling, but I've caught it right before curdling, so I'm counting that as a bonus for the day. Repositioning the pot on a cold burner to cool a bit, I turn my attention to measuring out the dry ingredients. My phone ringing catches me just as I'm measuring salt. I reach over to where it's sitting on the corner of the counter and hit the speaker button.

"Hello?"

"Em?"

"Hey, Bellamy. On your way to work?" I ask.

"Stuck in traffic as we speak. What are you up to?" she asks. "Savoring your life of leisure?"

I laugh and tip the salt into the mix.

"Something like that. Probably not as much as Creagan would want. Right now, I'm making cinnamon rolls," I tell her.

"You make cinnamon rolls?" she asks.

"I do when I'm in Sherwood. Yeast dough and all. Not a single exploding refrigerator can to be seen."

"It must be a special occasion," she says.

"Absolutely. I have a hot date with a game of Clue," I tell her.

"That… doesn't sound hot at all. You're terrible at that game."

I sigh and pour the warm milk into another bowl so I can add the yeast.

"As I've been told. If that damn Mr. Boddy would just stop pissing people off enough to get killed all the time, I wouldn't have to try to figure out which of his suspicious assortment of guests offed him."

"You know that's more disturbing when it's coming from you, right?" she asks.

"Probably."

"Anyway, I just wanted to let you know I forwarded you something. I forgot to tell you a couple days ago."

"What is it?" I ask.

"I don't know. It was just in your mail. It's a big envelope. I'd guess papers of some kind. It should get to you today," she says.

"Thanks. I appreciate you taking care of the house and everything, Bells."

"Not a problem. There are a couple of really cute officers assigned to the patrol there. Sometimes I go in just to flip lights on and off so I can look at them."

I laugh. "You have absolute permission to use any veiling tactic you'd like," I offer.

"I'll let you know if it does any good. Almost to work. Send me a cinnamon roll. Oh, and Emma?"

"Yes?"

"It was Ms. Scarlet in the lounge with the candlestick," she says.

"I knew I couldn't trust that bitch."

She laughs, and I end the call. I think I know what the papers are. I'm just not sure I'm ready to see them yet.

The dough is safely tucked away in the slightly heated oven under a damp towel when my phone rings again. I glance at the screen and smile at Sam's name.

"No need to prepare ways to tease me at the game tonight," I say by way of greeting. "I've got the game on lock. Bellamy already told me it was Ms. Scarlet in the lounge with the candlestick."

"Actually, it seems it was Ms. Zara in the bedroom with the rope," Sam mutters lowly. Seriously.

I pause as I tuck the bag of flour back into place in the pantry.

"What version are you playing? I don't remember that character. And I distinctly don't remember a bedroom. That's one of the issues I have with the mansion. No bedroom," I say.

"Unfortunately, I'm not playing anything. It's more serious than that," he tells me.

"What's going on?" I ask, the good feelings at him calling me draining away at the tightness in his voice.

"We just got a call from the housekeeper at the Blair Manor in Gracey Estates. She found Everly Zara's body about an hour ago. It looks like she killed herself."

My chest tightens. "That's horrible. Wait... Everly Zara. That name sounds familiar."

"It should. I'm already investigating the death of her stepdaughter."

CHAPTER FIVE

"Oh, god," I gasp as I remember the news reports over the last nearly three weeks.

"Yeah. So far, nobody has been able to get ahold of Michael Blair to notify him. The housekeeper screaming got the attention of his brother, but he's not answering his phone."

"His brother?" I ask. "Oh. That's right. He lives in the in-law suite."

"He does. And word is he isn't exactly crying rivers over his sister-in-law's death. But at least he's there for Maggie. She's apparently really shaken up," Sam says.

"I can imagine. That's an awful thing for her to find. So, I'm guessing you aren't going to be at game night this evening?" I ask.

"I don't know. I'm heading up there now to look at the scene and do some initial interviews. I need to try to get in touch with Blair so I can notify him before the media gets ahold of this. He's been through enough. The last thing he needs right now is to find out his wife is dead over a breaking news story."

"I can't even imagine how hard this is going to be for him."

"Neither can I. He hasn't been coping with his daughter's death well, and I know he and Everly weren't doing well since. He hasn't been back to the manor. This is going to hit him hard," he tells me.

"This is going to complicate the girl's investigation."

He lets out a deep sigh. "Yes, it is. Without her to give statements about what happened that night, there's not much to go on. That's another thing I'm going to have to talk to Michael Blair about when I finally find him."

"I'm sorry you're having to face that today," I say. "I'll miss you."

"Me too. What are you doing today?" he asks.

"Right now, I'm baking cinnamon rolls." He groans, and I can't help but laugh. "Then I have to go up to the management office."

"Management office?" he asks.

"For the house. Lionheart Property Management takes care of it and oversees the rentals."

"Why do you need to go there? If there are things that need to be fixed, I can do it for you."

I smile as I wipe off the table. "I know you can. And I will probably take you up on that with a couple of things. But that's not it. They actually called me yesterday and left a message saying they needed to talk to me. They asked if I'd come up to the office today," I explain.

"After I do everything else, I'm going to have a mountain of paperwork to do. But when that's done, I'll come by if it's not too late," he offers.

"It won't be too late. Just come over when you can."

I feel terrible for Sam as we get off the phone. His day is likely to be miserable, and the chances of them getting better over the next couple of weeks probably aren't good. I haven't been involved in the investigation into the death of the young boy, so there are details he hasn't shared with me. From what I know, this suicide is only going to make it more complicated.

Turning on the TV in my bedroom as I get dressed only confirms it. A shaky image of a sprawling estate on a manicured hill seems to come from a news helicopter. It shows emergency vehicles dotting the long driveway and blocking the end, so media vehicles can't get closer. Police roam the grass and come in and out of the house. Sam isn't there yet, but I know when he gets there, he'll be furious to see the media. He hates how they descend on scenes like vultures, picking for the scraps of anything they can exploit. It's especially bad in situations like this when all the details aren't known, and there hasn't been proper notification.

But as long as they don't say her name, they aren't technically doing anything wrong. It could be anyone dead in the exquisite manor owned by Michael Blair, the wealthiest man in Sherwood and probably quite a distance beyond. But it isn't just anyone. It's Everly Zara, the beautiful young woman Blair married less than three months ago. Very little is known about her. She doesn't come from any of the highly publicized socialite families or have any links to wealth and power the way people would expect in the wife of someone like Blair.

Instead, she comes from a modest immigrant family. Came. She *came* from a modest immigrant family from Europe. Just that slight shift of the word makes so much of an impact. I stop and look at the screen again. The footage is live, showing the chaos surrounding the house. She's still in there. It all happened so quickly that her body still hasn't been taken out by the coroner. Sam mentioned a rope, which means she hanged herself. I've seen several instances when the body is not cut down immediately but left in place for sometimes hours after discovery to ensure the proper pictures and notes are taken. Considering Sam hasn't arrived on the scene yet, that is likely the case today.

It's eerie to look at the screen knowing that. I wonder which of the windows across the top of the house is the bedroom and hope it's been covered. I've been with law enforcement long enough to know people will stop at nothing to get an exclusive picture or detail in a case like this. The more shocking and grisly, the better. Now that the news of a body in the manor is out, I wouldn't put it past any of the media to try to sneak a shot of her.

The image on the screen mercifully changes over to a photo of Everly Zara and Michael Blair the night of their engagement. Smiling as she displayed her new ring with her hand resting on her Blair's chest, Everly looked every inch the gorgeous socialite wife. Thick, glossy hair swept up at the back of her head, showed off her graceful neck and her glittering silver dress. Blair wore a meticulously tailored dark suit and a look of sheer love and adoration as he gazed at Everly.

They looked happy and content in a way that makes it unfathomable how much everything would change in just a few short weeks.

As the image shifts up into the top corner of the screen and the rest returns to the stream of the house, the voice-over reminds viewers of the rest of the woman's sad story. Only weeks after celebrating their private elopement with hundreds of people at a lavish party Blair planned for her, he had to leave town for a short business trip. Usually, his young daughter Penelope would go to her mother's house, and Everly would travel with Michael, but this time Payton wasn't able to take the two-year-old. Everly agreed to watch the little girl, and because she always got along wonderfully with his daughter, Michael agreed.

Just four hours after Blair left the house, emergency responders got a frantic call from Everly. She said Penelope wasn't breathing. She hit her head while playing and wouldn't wake up. They found her on the floor and brought her to the hospital where she lay in critical condition for several long, painful days before finally dying. There was heavy suggestion of the circumstances being suspicious and continuous innuendo since the day she was hurt, but nothing has come of it. Sam tells me things look strange, and he can't fully sign off on it being an accident, but also has no concrete evidence of it being anything else. He was preparing for another interview with Everly in the coming week.

Now it will never happen.

The full story of what actually happened that night and how Penelope ended up on the marble floor went with her.

CHAPTER SIX

FIVE YEARS AGO

He reached over and took her hand as the car drove up to a massive iron gate set in a large stone wall. She would always remember that. It tightened around hers as the gate opened and he drove slowly onto the cobblestone path beyond. It felt like excitement, like he couldn't wait to finally be bringing her here after talking about it for days. But there was also the sense of holding her still.

"I've seen this place before," she told him. "I've driven by a couple times. I never knew what it was."

He flashed her a smile. No words, just that smile. As they continued down the cobblestones, she looked through the window beside her. Around them, beautiful, carefully landscaped grounds stretched out within the confines of the wall like a secret garden. Tall trees created blissful pockets of shade. Emerald grass was trimmed to absolute precision around lush flowerbeds and bubbling fountains.

Outside the stone barrier was gray and bleak. Block buildings stacked up on cement pads and trash piled up in narrow alleyways. Miserable people, rushed lives. Gutters washing hope and ambition into the sewers with the rain.

That all fell away here. The metal gate seemed almost ominous from the outside, but when it closed behind her, it felt like protection. She didn't have to think about anything that disappointed and hurt her. She didn't have to think about the struggles and difficulty she went through as she tried to claw her way from the meager beginnings her parents gave her. They did all they could for her. But she always knew there was more. There was something else waiting for her. She just had to find it.

She had been fighting to do just that since she could fake her age convincingly enough to get a job. Progress was slow, and all the fighting was wearing her down. But here, beyond the wall, it felt like she didn't have to fight. This seemed like a place where people could thrive. This was a place unlike any she had ever been. She already never wanted to leave.

The car stopped at a small building at the edge of the path. There was no barrier or bar of any kind to stop them, but the presence of the building was enough. He rolled down the window and smiled out at an older man who stepped out of the building and stood at the edge of the path.

"Jeremiah, it's good to see you," the older man said.

It struck her as odd. That wasn't his name. At least, that wasn't what she called him.

"Good to see you as well. I have a friend I'd like to introduce to Lucas."

"He'll be glad to hear that," the older man said and gestured for them to continue on.

She wanted to ask him about his name as they continued along the cobblestone path, but something stopped her. It's like the surroundings themselves kept the words from coming out of her mouth. She didn't want to ruin the serene beauty of the secret garden she had only just discovered. If she said anything, the bubble might burst, the protection might vanish. She couldn't risk it. She didn't know what this place was or what it offered her, but she was already terrified to lose it.

The woman who came out of the next little building they encountered peered through the open window at her with a warm, welcoming smile.

"If you stay for a little while, I will be off duty later. I would love to meet you."

He nodded. "We'll be here."

They drove to the back of the building, and he pulled into a low, rectangular building to park among several other cars. He only released her hand when he had to get out of the car, then took it up again as soon as he opened her door. She felt suddenly nervous as he led her toward the large arched wooden door in the back of the tall stone building. The positioning of the building on the grounds meant it wasn't visible from the street. It rose up in front of them as they came down the cobblestones, and now that she was standing behind it, she could see it in its full glory.

It looked like a castle, a palace holding something beautiful and secret, exclusive and hidden. Her body tingled as she realized she was being granted entry. He was bringing her not just to the door, but beyond it. What the miserable and beaten down outside the wall would never know even existed; she would experience with her own eyes.

They walked through the door, and he led her down a hallway lined with candles. It made her want to whisper and walk closer beside him. The further they went, the farther she felt from the rest of the world. Finally, they made it to a large room. It was completely round, and the door they walked through was the only entrance or exit. There were no windows, only large, beautiful paintings that underlined the feeling that they had walked into a true castle. He led her to a couch positioned beside a table and gestured for her to sit down. Silver platters and tiered stands on the table displayed chocolates and delicate looking treats. They were too lovely and perfect to be real. But he reached out for one and held it to her lips.

"Eloise is the most incredible cook. It may be a good thing I'm not always here, or I would never stop eating."

She opened her mouth and let him place the decadent chocolate on her tongue. The bite melted into silky, rich flavors that made her eyes close and a sigh escape her lips. When she opened them again, he was finishing the other half of the chocolate. There was something intimate in that, a message that locked her a little closer to him.

"Are you here often?" she asked.

He nodded. "Yes. But not nearly as much as I want to be. I hope to change that soon."

"What is this place?"

She asked it in a whisper. Everything around her still felt fragile. It couldn't be real, but she wanted to drift in the dream as long as she could. If she said something wrong, it could all shatter around her like sugar-glass, and the world she knew would come back.

"Have you ever felt like you didn't fit in with other people? Like the world didn't really understand you?" he asked.

It was like hearing her own words come out of his mouth. It took her breath away.

"Yes," she finally answered when she found her voice again.

"It's like you were created for something more. You were born into a place that wasn't yours and have been looking for where you would fit."

She nodded. "Yes."

He reached out and ran his fingers along the side of her face. The touch made her skin warm and her heart skip. It craved affection. She ached for validation, for acknowledgement, for touch. She leaned her face into his hand, and he let her cheek rest in his palm.

"You were. I know you were. Just like I was."

The door opened, and the woman from the second small building came in. Her smile widened when she saw her sitting there. She rushed forward with her arms open and gathered her into a hug that brought her off the couch. It felt warm and soft, comforting and reassuring in a way she had never experienced. She never wanted to step out of that hug. When the woman stepped back, she turned to him.

"Jeremiah, she's such a beauty. I know the Elders will be pleased to meet her."

He nodded. "She was just telling me she feels that she has never fit in and that she is meant for something more."

34

The way he turned the conversation placed the ownership of the words into her hands. Though he was the one who asked the questions and guided her to her admissions, he offered the power back to her. He held her up as the one in control. The woman's eyes widened, and she nodded enthusiastically.

"Of course. It is so clear." She took both her hands in hers. "You see, most people are the same. They have their roles, and they live their lives without ever wondering if there's something more. For nearly all of them, there isn't. But there is a very select few, a precious chosen number, who know there's more. It is up to them, up to us, to prepare the way for achieving what is possible."

The door opened again, and an older woman walked in alongside a tall man with streaks of gray through his hair.

"Lucas," he said, his voice filled with respect for the older man.

Lucas stopped when he saw her.

"It's you," he said.

It took her aback. She looked at the others before looking into the older man's eyes again.

"Excuse me?" she asked.

"You. I would know you anywhere. We've been waiting for you, Sister Abigail."

CHAPTER SEVEN

NOW

I went to the management office with my father one time before leaving Sherwood. He was in the process of buying the house near school and knew we didn't need my grandparents' house anymore. But he wasn't going to get rid of it. I didn't fully understand it at the time. The older I get, the more sense it makes. We were always running when I was young. It felt like something they were doing to me, that somehow I was the reason for it. Now I recognize they were running just as much as I was. It might have been their choice, but that doesn't mean it wasn't hard on them.

Keeping the house rather than just selling it was his way of holding on to something. Sherwood was an anchor for him as well.

Very little has changed since coming here with him. That day he was making arrangements for the company to care for the house and find renters. I waited outside the private office, reading slightly outdated magazines and subtly listening in to the conversations going on around me. I could only hear half of the phone calls, but my mind filled in the rest.

My curiosity and imagination sometimes got me in trouble, but it also kept me entertained. I didn't recognize it in myself then that I was already focusing in on details, drawing out hidden elements of what I observed, and retaining them. It would become invaluable for my career. That afternoon it just introduced me to the surprisingly complex web of Sherwood's romance world. Including one secretary's affair with the wife of one of the owners.

That's the one I was always interested in finding out how it all turned out. Not well is my assumption, but stranger things have happened.

I park in the parking lot that looks essentially the same as it did that afternoon. Not that terribly much can change about a parking lot. The layout and minimalist decor of the office also looks the same. But it immediately strikes me that the space doesn't look worn down or tired, like it needs a refresh. Instead, it looks carefully maintained, consistent, and predictable. There's a subtle underlying message in that. This company is reliable. You can depend on them to take care of your property and never surprise you.

One of the women at the handful of desks taking up the front portion of the building looks up as I walk through the glass door. She smiles.

"Hey, Emma. It's good to see you," she says.

I very highly doubt the sincerity of that statement. I was in two classes with her in high school, and there was a brief rivalry over Sam. At least, she engaged in a brief rivalry. I barely acknowledged she was even around until the rumors got vicious. We moved again only a few weeks later. I'm guessing she's one of the people who pushed my existence out of their minds and barely remembered me until I got back and people started talking.

"Hi, Pamela. I got a message from Derrick yesterday asking me to come in. Is he available?" I ask.

She gestured toward the partially closed office door at the back of the room.

"Should be right in there. Go ahead back. How's it been being back? Everything okay with the house?"

I had taken a step toward the office, but I stop and look back at her.

"The house is fine. Still getting used to a few changes and things, but it's pretty much like I remember," I tell her.

"And you're... feeling better?" she asks.

Her head tilts slightly down, so she peers at me through the tops of her eyes. It's the kind of look someone gives you when you're having a conversation they think is secretive, but is just awkward.

"Feeling better?" I ask.

"Well, yeah," she says, resting her elbows on the desk and leaning a little closer. "I heard you came back here because... well... you know."

Her mouth pulls into a thin line, and her eyes widen briefly. The universal expression for someone who wants to say something but doesn't want to say it. I cock my hip and cross my arms over my stomach.

"Actually, no. I don't know. Why is it I came back here?"

Pamela shifts in her seat. "I just heard that case you did earlier this year really got to you. That it broke you down and maybe you weren't... all yourself anymore. So, you came here to put the pieces back together."

Part of the motivation for the change of venue for Jake Logan's trial was my identity being leaked and the disruption that ensued. It didn't surprise me. It was most likely going to come out eventually anyway. It's the death threats I could do without. The police suggested it gave some explanation for the intruder in my house, but I doubt it. The strange issues started well before my name and picture got attached to Jake's case. But the link obviously did its work in the rumor mill. Pamela is looking at me like she's trying to needle something out of me for book club gossip fodder.

"I came here because the sheriff asked for my help after Alice Brooks, Caleb Donahue, and Eva Francis were kidnapped," I tell her firmly. "Excuse me."

Without giving her a chance to respond, I stalk through the lobby to the office. Derrick Marmion looks up from his desk when I rap lightly on the door.

"Emma, hi," he nods, gesturing at the chair across the desk from him. "Thanks for coming in. Have a seat."

"Hi, Derrick," I say as I lower myself into the chair. "I got your message yesterday. You sounded kind of concerned. Is everything alright with the house?"

"Everything is fine with the house," he reassures me. "At least, as far as I know. Have you had any problems while you've been back?"

"Just a few minor little things. Nothing to be worried about," I tell him.

"If there's something wrong, we'll take care of it. That's why we're here. I can get you in touch with our maintenance team, and they'll schedule an appointment to come—"

I hold up my hand to stop him. "Really. It's fine. But thank you for the offer." Clancy back in Feathered Nest was perfectly nice, but the thought of another maintenance man coming into my house isn't something I'm too keen on right now. "If the house is fine, why did you need me to come up here?"

"Unfortunately, it looks like there's a possibility there might have been an attempted break-in at the storage unit," Derrick says.

My mind sifts through all the ambiguous statements to try to figure out what he's talking about. I shake my head, not coming up with anything.

"Storage unit?" I frown. "What storage unit?"

"Your father didn't tell you about it when he transferred control to you?" he asks.

I shake my head again, swallowing down the emotions that question brings up. The papers transferring ownership of the Sherwood house to me weren't with the other papers I got when my father disappeared. They showed up later, sent by the management company without pomp and circumstance as if it were completely normal for an eighteen-year-old to suddenly have control over a rental property. In so many ways, it was even harder to look at those papers. The house near college could be a gift. An investment into my burgeoning adulthood. But my father loved the house in Sherwood. Holding the deed to that in my hands and seeing my name on it was terrifyingly final.

"No," I tell him.

"When your father first decided to have this company take over management of the house, there were some items left in the attic and storage space. He asked us to store them and use the fund left for the maintenance of the house to pay for the fees until he came back for the items. Since he has not returned for them, we've been paying for the unit since."

He looks down at his desk as he talks about my father not returning, glossing over the sentence like he doesn't even want to say it. No one in Sherwood knows the full story of what happened to my father. No one but Sam. He's the only one who was there when it happened and knows there's more to it than him just no longer being around. I'm sure there are stories and rumors. He's probably been crafted into some sort of folklore character around here. I haven't heard any of the stories. I'm glad. I don't know how I would react.

"I didn't know about it. You say it's been broken into?" I ask.

He nods regretfully.

"At least, someone tried. It doesn't look like they got all the way inside. But the door and lock are damaged. I wanted to make sure you knew so you could check the contents," he tells me.

"I don't even know what's in there," I point out.

"I still suggest you take a look and let us know if it seems anyone has gained access."

It's the plea of a company that doesn't want to be held legally responsible for a failure in security. He reaches in his desk drawer and pulls out a pair of keys hanging from a ring with a large white rubber number marker on it. He holds them out to me, and I take them.

"Do you have any idea who might have tried to get inside?" I ask. "Aren't there security measures in place?"

His face goes slightly paler, but he doesn't let his smile drop.

"Yes. The storage units are behind a large gate with code access. The code is on the back of the keychain, by the way. Unfortunately, it is possible to climb over the fence surrounding the entire grounds."

"There aren't any surveillance cameras?"

"Only on the front gate."

41

I nod. "Maybe something you should look into. Thank you. I'll let you know when I've checked the unit."

Derrick stands and offers his hand. I shake it and head out of the building without casting a look toward Pamela. Outside, the rain has started to fall again, and I duck my head to keep it from my face. I get into the car and lean my head back against the seat with a heavy sigh.

Glancing down at the keys in my hand, I debate going straight to the unit or finishing my other errands for the day. Curiosity wins out. I rev the engine and head for the storage company on the other side of town.

CHAPTER EIGHT

I'm not sure what to expect when I pull up to the fence surrounding the storage unit and type in the code written on the back of the key tag. The gate shivers and groans before finally relenting and opening slowly enough for me to want to drive forward well before it's open. I have no idea what might be in the unit waiting for me, and I'm more curious by the second. I wonder why my father never told me about the things left behind in the house. I don't understand why he wouldn't come back and get them or ask for them to be sent to us. The amount spent on the rental fees for the unit could easily have covered shipping to us.

When the gate finally opens, I drive through and follow the signs bolted into the sides of the cement buildings to the back bank of units. It's only a few dozen yards away from the fence surrounding the grounds. Whoever tried to break into the unit only had to climb the chain link, hop down, and cross a section of pavement I doubt gets seen more than a handful of times each week, if that. Two light poles tower on either corner of the parking lot, but their tiny, angled heads likely only create pools of light that stretch a few feet around them to either side.

"Not even giving you an A for effort," I mutter as I climb out of the car and walk up to the door to the unit.

I see the signs of damage Derrick mentioned at the office. It's clear someone took some sort of tool to the door and to the lock itself. Someone put a lot of effort into breaking that lock before something scared them away. Or maybe they just gave up. Either way, they didn't get inside, which leaves the mysteries inside to me.

During the few times I ventured into the attic when I was younger, I was more invested in finding a hiding spot than paying attention to what was around me. The nooks and crannies were great for curling up with a baggie of snacks and a book, but I don't remember what made them. I can't think of what they would have left behind to end up stashed away back here for years. I've never had a storage unit, so my only personal frame of reference is movies and TV shows. Which, of course, means I'm envisioning stacks of nonsensical furniture and endless towers of cardboard boxes.

I don't know if I'm relieved or disappointed when I open the door and there's one old chair and a few plastic totes. It looks like my grandparents took some time to condense their belongings and trade out their old cardboard boxes. As I run my hand over the top box, imagining my grandmother packing it, it hits me, she isn't the one who left it and the others behind. It was years between my grandparents' deaths and my father giving control of the house over to the management company. My grandmother would have no way of knowing the items in these boxes were going to be left or put into storage, which means it had to be my father who did it.

But why? Why these things? I still remember when my grandmother died, following my grandfather only a few months after his death. We went to the house and cleared all of their personal possessions out. I remember how empty it felt when we opened the door, and I knew I wouldn't smell my grandmother's perfume or my grandfather's pipe tobacco wafting out to welcome me in. There would be no biscuits and gravy for breakfast or overflowing bowl of fruit in the middle of the kitchen counter that looked too pretty to disrupt but was so delicious on a hot afternoon. Somehow that was sadder than when we finished taking the clothes out of the bedroom closets and dropped her toiletries into the trash. Her shampoo bottle was nearly full. I'll never forget that.

Even after I left Sherwood for the last time, never intending on going back, I figured my father would. That house meant so much to him, and I knew he would make his way back there some time. When he told me it was becoming a rental property, I never wondered about the possessions still in the house. Over the years, pieces of their furniture ended up in our house and pictures appeared on the walls. Dad would come back from a visit with boxes to go through so he could gradually dismantle the existence of the house frozen in place when my grandparents died. It never occurred to me that he chose to leave some things there.

Taking the top off the first box, I glance inside. It's an assortment of old Christmas decorations. They don't match the tree my father always put up each year, meticulously arranged, so it looked like the front of a magazine. I also don't remember any of them from the holidays we got to spend with my grandparents. There aren't many of those in my childhood. It seems like while everyone else heads for their families' homes for Thanksgiving or Christmas, for us, it meant steering clear. When my father disappeared, I started to wonder if not being with my grandparents at the holidays was because of him. Not because he didn't want to be with them, but because someone would expect us to be there.

After going through the Christmas decorations, I check my phone. Much more time has passed between my meeting with Derrick and going through the storage unit than I expected. I still have several things I need to do before getting back to the house to pop the cinnamon rolls into the oven and head across the street for game night. I hate the thought of Sam not being there. But I know he's doing what he has to do. And if Janet chooses Monopoly for tonight, him not being there means I can snag the top hat.

Deciding I'll come back later when I have more time, I put the top back on the box and close the storage unit door. The new lock I bought on the way here is bigger and stronger than the original lock. It clicks solidly into place, and I give it a tug for good measure. I'm satisfied with myself, but a crawling feeling up the back of my neck from the fence tempts me to turn around. The fence and the tree line behind it are unchanged. There's no indication of where the person came over the fence or if they came out of the woods. It's entirely possible they just walked around from the front of the building and followed the fence until they came to the shadowy space between the two light poles.

I glance at each corner of the building. Metal braces bolt small black cameras to each corner, pointed so they would cover the entire space in front of the units. Derrick told me the units weren't covered by security cameras, that the only cameras were the ones at the front gate recording the people going in and out. That means the cameras on the corners of the building are dummies. That's not all that uncommon. Most people would be shocked to know just how much of the security they see in public places is nothing more than props. Reflective domes on store ceilings housing nothing, stickers proclaiming protection from alarm systems that don't actually exist, prominently positioned security offices more likely to contain coats and set-aside merchandise than officers.

They act as a form of behavior control. People are less likely to take a risk of doing something illegal if they think strong measures are in place to snare them. Creating the idea of security is often just as effective as actually having it. Except in this circumstance. It would have been nice for those plastic shells to actually contain recording technology.

Ticking off the next few items on my to-do list takes me right up to the time when I need to get my cinnamon rolls baking. I grab a few bags out of my backseat and head for the front door. When I get to the front porch, I look over at the neighbor's yard again.

A flicker of black goes around the corner of the house. It might have been a dog, or a shadow, or even my imagination. But I don't think it was. It looked like the man I saw earlier. The man who I couldn't have seen.

Yet I know I did. He was right there, standing at the corner of the yard and staring back at me. And in that brief moment, my heart stopped. Because I knew his eyes.

They were exactly like my own.

CHAPTER NINE

HIM

He pressed back against the wall and waited. He'd learned the patterns of the people who lived in this house and knew they wouldn't notice him dropping down into the rounded cinderblock vault surrounding the basement window. The spot had become his refuge, his hiding place when eyes lingered too long on him.

Like hers. He knew she saw him. That morning and just moments ago. He couldn't help it. As much as he told himself he had to be careful and stay away from her, to keep his distance until the right time, it was getting harder. It seemed like the more he saw her, the more drawn to her he was. It happened so long ago. All he wanted was to go to her. But she wouldn't know what to do if he did. It would be too dangerous. For both of them, really. Especially now. His last plan was an incredible disaster, and he was still trying to pick up the pieces. When he found out what happened, he would ensure the ones responsible were punished. It was his most basic principle. Wrath before death. He learned it fast, and he learned it well.

For now, he would concentrate on Emma. She was still in Sherwood, still in the house he never thought she would step foot in again. There were no signs of the old hesitation on her face when she walked up the steps and through the front door. Her hand didn't shake. Her body stayed relaxed. She clicked back into place easily in the weeks she spent here. It made him uneasy.

This wasn't where she belonged. Of course, there was a time when more people thought she did than didn't. They saw her on the sidewalks. Waited on her in the diner. Cleaned her dropped popcorn off the movie theater floor. Graded her papers. She was one of many, and because of that, they had no question this was where she fit. But she wasn't one of many. In the entire world, there was just one. Only her. And she was so much more than just another ripple in the slow-moving water.

They didn't know what made her extraordinary. How could they? She didn't even know. But she would. One day. One day soon, she would know that she was set aside for something more than she could have ever imagined. More than the world could imagine.

As he stood in the stone vault to wait, he glanced in the basement window. Not all the houses around here had basements, but the ones that did fascinate him. They struck him as something from another time. Attics made sense to him. Stashing away unneeded items away in the top floor of the house was like tucking thoughts into the back of your mind. They were still there. Not really hidden, only put out of sight until they were needed again. An attic was memories. Not always good. Not always ones you wanted to explore again. But important enough to be set aside and kept close.

A basement brought to mind fear. It was a hiding place. Basements were where you fled to weather a storm, when the threat of the wind and destruction outweighed the gloom. Secrets were kept in basements. Ones cast into corners to be forgotten. Ones left to disintegrate. Ones that breathed. Kept underfoot. They weren't a part of life.

That wasn't every basement, of course. Some pretended their basements were extensions of their homes. Curtains in the below-ground windows. Painted walls to take away the dank. Furniture scattered in spaces with glaring bulbs to chase away the shadows. They opened the door to the rest of their home and let the life of the upper floors flow down.

The basement of this house was so dark he could barely see anything. Not enough sunlight filtered through the uncovered glass to illuminate what was stored there, and the dark forms hunkering among support columns could be monsters.

He was drawn into the image of the basement so much he nearly lost the time. He had to time himself carefully, so she wouldn't see him again. Another glimpse might make it less likely she would leave the house. He needed her gone. Not for long. Just long enough for him to get inside.

She was at the storage unit earlier. He caught her there only by chance. The woods had become another useful spot, a place he could stay for the hours he needed to be away from the main streets but didn't want to be too far away. No one ever went in except for teenagers looking for a place to drink and have sex where they wouldn't be seen. He hazarded getting close to the fence surrounding the lot, so he could look at the unit again. He shouldn't have. By now, the manager would have called the police to tell them about the man he found trying to break in and nearly caught. Them keeping an eye on the area was probably the same thing that made the teenagers who called attention to him flee from the trees.

It was a transaction. They traded him for their own reputation. Sounding the alarm when they saw him hop over the fence and run for the unit was admitting they were in the trees, but that didn't sink in for the manager. He only knew they called frantically, and he got to the back of the buildings in time to stop the intrusion before the lock hit the ground. The manager wouldn't think about the parties in the trees now. It was curtains on a basement window.

He didn't watch her long. Just long enough to know she got inside. If she took anything, he needed to know. And he needed to get it.

When enough time passed, so he was sure she was inside, he climbed back out onto the lawn and walked casually away. He'd come back later when the darkness would let him slip inside. He wondered if the brick beside the back door was still loose and if he'd find the key behind it.

He did his best to stay at the outer edge of the properties he crossed. He wasn't expecting the older man clearing a section of ground large enough to be a garden. Making it bare now would make it easier to plant when the warm weather came and thawed the winter freeze to come. He pressed on a little faster when he saw him, hoping the man was lost enough in his work not to notice him. He didn't pause when he heard the man's voice. The name he called bounced off him and fell to the grass. He left it there.

CHAPTER TEN

I've never been one for conspiracy theories. People with their heads wrapped in aluminum foil and spouting out their views on why the various races of aliens are our clear and unquestioned superiors don't really sit well with me. But I leave Janet and Paul's house with my own new conspiracy theory. My neighbors and the man I'm dating are conspiring to undermine my ability to unravel a murder mystery one game of Clue at a time.

It's probably not that serious. But I couldn't help but notice they put away the game when I arrived without Sam. On the other hand, I went on to dominate at The Game of Life. I'm sure there's something poetic and symbolic in that, but frankly, I'm too stuffed full of cinnamon rolls and Janet's walnut brownies to be terribly philosophical at this moment. The evening hasn't quite slipped into full-on darkness when I cross the street back toward my house. It's that brief time of day when the air looks blue and soft, almost like you could gather a handful of it.

I haven't heard from Sam yet. But I told him I would be waiting for him no matter what the time, so I plan on taking up real estate on the couch and tuning in to whatever true crime show happens to be on. He tells me he hates when I watch those shows. I'm on a break; he reminds me. I'm supposed to be giving my mind a break and recovering. It's not good for me. But I love them. I love the puzzle, the rush of watching the criminals fall. Sometimes I get the silly thrill of seeing a case I worked on, or watch Eric or Bellamy do an interview about one of their cases. I can only imagine this is something like what football fans feel when they're watching a game. Maybe I need a jersey to wear while I cheer on the home team. My black FBI t-shirt just doesn't really cut it.

Depending on how long it takes Sam to get here, I might be able to indulge in a few episodes before he gets there to scold me. Unless it's a show that catches his attention. He doesn't think I've noticed him watching at the same time he's telling me I shouldn't be. It would be adorable if it wasn't aggravating. It might still be a little adorable.

Before I open the door, I notice a thick manila envelope sitting on my porch. It was either delivered after I left for game night, or I just didn't notice it in my rush to get inside this afternoon. Scooping it up, I carry it inside and toss it onto the coffee table before heading into my bedroom. Freshly showered and changed into one of those delightful outfits that can double as casual clothes and pajamas, I walk back into the living room through long shadows coming into the windows. The cinnamon rolls are still with me, but a steaming cup of coffee will see me through however long I need to wait for Sam.

I curl up on the couch and stare at the envelope sitting on the table, waiting for me. Bellamy's smooth, swirling handwriting across the front confirms these are the papers she redirected to me after they arrived at my house. I know what they are without even having to open the outer envelope. It's why I haven't picked it up yet.

It's not that I don't want to know what's inside. After all, I'm the one who requested the documents and other records when I was in Iowa. There are things in there I need to know. But that's just the thing. I don't know them. Right now, I'm in a bit of a standoff. Right now, those papers could say anything. They could be whatever I want them to be. As soon as I open that envelope, I'll know. I'll know the secrets those papers hold, and I will never be able to return to the time when I didn't know them.

It would be easier if the envelope was thin. If it was just a couple of pieces of paper or a letter saying the Department of Vital Statistics hasn't been able to find anything, I would be in the same place I've been in. It would be frustrating, but no more frustrating than every other day that passes when I don't know something more about what happened to my mother, or where my father went the day he disappeared. But the envelope is thick and heavy. I can't genuinely hope Bellamy wrapped the original in bubble wrap before chucking it into her own envelope and addressing it to me. It means the search into the records came up with more than I ever could have imagined.

As soon as I open it, everything will change.

I drain half my coffee before feeling steady enough to pick up the envelope. Not giving myself time to hesitate anymore, I tear the flap open and let the inner envelope slide out. The handwriting with my address is shaky, but the Iowa return address is in a blue stamp positioned at a slight angle, like it was done hastily. Tearing it open, I pull out the stack of papers and set the envelope aside.

The first document on the stack makes my breath catch in my throat. It doesn't loosen as I flip through more. I'm halfway through the stack when I get up from the couch and go back into my bedroom for my phone. It rings three times before a muffled voice answers.

"'lo?"

"Are you eating?" I ask.

A gulping sound follows a brief pause.

"Egg salad on rye," Eric says.

"That sounds like an elegant dinner," I comment.

"Nothing but luxury for me. Tonight, it's fine dining at an exclusive little spot called my desk."

"Hard to get a reservation there?"

"Unfortunately, not particularly. I've been a regular customer pretty much non-stop for the last couple of weeks. But I'm willing to take an intermission for you. What's up?" he asks.

"I need you to look into a few things for me," I tell him.

"It's never a good thing when you say that."

"Just listen. I got the papers from Iowa."

"Anything interesting?" he asks.

I take a breath. "You could say that. Turns out, that's where my father was born. And I think I lived there for a while."

"Oh," Eric says.

He makes a few sounds like he's hoping they'll eventually bring themselves together into cohesive words. When they don't, I cut back in.

"There are some newspaper clippings and a few other things. I'm going to send them to you. Can you do your magic for me?" I ask.

"What am I looking for?"

"Anything. Whatever you can find that has anything to do with... anything."

"Thank you for narrowing that down for me," Eric says through another bite of sandwich.

"I'm sorry. I don't have much more than that to go on. But we've been trying to figure out why that hotel registration card pointed to Iowa. Now we know. Maybe this is how we find Ron Murdock."

"It's worth a shot," he says. "You know I'm in. Whatever you need, you've got. Give me just a few days."

"Thanks, I appreciate ..."

My voice trails off.

"Emma? Is something wrong?"

The sound that stopped me happens again. It's coming from the back of the house, a low scraping.

"I thought I heard something," I tell Eric, lowering my voice slightly as I move toward the sound.

"What is it?"

"It sounds like someone's trying to open my back door."

"With you inside?"

"The lights are all off," I explain.

The sound makes my skin burn, and it's harder to get my breaths in and out of my lungs. I force my feet to keep moving toward the back door even though the memories in the back of my mind tell me to run out the front. I fight the flashes. I fight the sound of crackling flames and the bite of cold. Jake's face forms in front of my eyes, and I squeeze them closed to melt him away.

"Can you see anybody?" Eric asks.

It makes me open my eyes and continue toward the back door. The sound is louder as I move toward the kitchen, but it goes quiet when I get into the room.

"No," I tell him. "I don't hear it anymore. But I know someone was there."

"You need to call the police."

I head toward my bedroom, but a figure at the open front door stops me. Gasping, I stumble back a step before the face registers. I let out a breath and lift my voice a little louder to get over Eric's frantic rambling.

"I don't need to call the police. They're already here," I say.

"What?"

"It's Sam," I tell him.

"Tell him I'm going to kick his ass if he does that again." He pauses. "Actually, no. Don't tell him that."

I give a shaky laugh. "Give me a call if you find anything, okay?"

"Want me to see if I can snag you a reservation at my exclusive restaurant?" he asks.

"Soon."

"Night, Em."

CHAPTER ELEVEN

My hand shakes as I end the call. I try to stuff my phone into my pocket before I remember my stretchy leggings don't have pockets. Sam closes the front door and comes toward me.

"Emma?" he asks.

My body sways slightly when he grabs my shoulders, and I have the urge to sit down, but I shake it off.

"What were you doing?" I ask.

Sam narrows his eyes at me. "What? What do you mean? I told you I was coming tonight after I finished up for the day. You said it wouldn't be too late. Did you forget?"

"No," I say, shaking my head. "I knew you were coming. But why did you go to the back door?"

His eyes narrow. "The back door? I didn't go to the back door."

My stomach sinks. "You weren't at the back door a few minutes ago?"

"No. I just got here. Someone was at your back door?"

He moves me out of his way and walks around me to go into the kitchen to the back door. I follow close behind him, going back over what I heard in my mind.

"I thought I heard someone. I was on the phone with Eric, and it sounded like someone was scraping at the back door. I went in there, but it stopped," I tell him.

Sam moves aside the curtain hanging over the glass portion of the back door and looks around.

"You didn't see anyone?" he asks.

"No. The back porch light burned out, and I haven't replaced it. In the dark, I couldn't see any silhouette against the curtain."

He turns the lock and opens the door. Taking a step out onto the small back porch, he looks around again.

"You need better locks on this door," he mutters. "Thumb turns like this aren't secure. You need a deadbolt that requires a key. I'll get one at the hardware store tomorrow and put it in for you."

"I can change my own locks," I snap at him. He doesn't even react. "It's not like it would be the first time."

He looks at me over his shoulder, his eyes dark.

"Come look at this," he says.

I step outside with him, and he points to the brick side of the porch. One of the bricks is out of place. It's not much, just barely pulled forward. The difference is so slight no one would notice it unless they knew to look for it. But Sam does. And so do I.

"Is there still a key there?" he asks.

I shake my head. "No. There hasn't been a key hidden in there since the management company took over and started renting out the house. At least, not as far as I know. I checked it when I first got here, just to see if anybody else used my old hiding place, but it was empty. It could be out of place just because I didn't push it back in all the way."

"Or it could be someone who would know to look for the key behind that brick," he muses. "I'm going to call the station. A couple of the boys can come out here and investigate, make sure it's all on record and everything."

I shake my head and take hold of his hand, pulling him toward me.

"No. We don't need to do all that," I tell him.

"Emma, someone was trying to get into your house," he says.

"Maybe," I admit. "But I didn't see anything. Neither did you, and you were right out front. Maybe my mind really is slipping. Come on, let's just go inside."

He doesn't seem completely convinced, but he lets me guide him in and lock the door behind us.

"At least let me change that light for you. Do you have any bulbs?" he asks.

"If I do, they're in the cabinet above the washing machine."

He nods and heads for the laundry room as I make another cup of coffee. The half one still left in the living room is cold by now, and a chill has settled into my bones. Now that Sam's here, I don't really need the caffeine to keep me humming through the night, but I need to warm up from the inside. Sam fixes the light and comes into the living room, sitting beside me where I'm curled under a blanket in the corner of the couch.

"Are you going to tell me what that crack about your mind slipping was supposed to mean?" he asks.

I take a sip of my coffee. "Nothing."

"It's obviously something if you think you were conjuring someone trying to get into your house," he says.

"I had to go up to the management office today, and I saw Pamela Bryan," I finally explain.

"Welsh. It's Pamela Welsh, now. I guess. At least it was before they got divorced."

"Well, whatever her last name is, she took it upon herself to let me know people think I came back here because I lost my mind," I tell him.

"What?" he asks.

"Yep," I say with a slow nod. "Apparently, the word around the old grapevine is I slunk back home to lick my wounds and piece my shattered sanity back together. I'm just too fragile to keep working with the Bureau, which is why I haven't left."

"Was she wearing a skintight leopard print dress and holding a cigarette holder at the time she told you that?" Sam asks with a glint in his eye.

"As enthralling as that visual of the suburbanite gossip was, I think you're missing the point," I say.

He slides closer to me. "No, I'm not. But you don't need to listen to her. People talk. It's what they do. Especially when you've lived in the same place for your entire life and might have the slight notion that nothing actually exists beyond the borders."

"I wouldn't know how that feels," I say.

Sam strokes a piece of hair behind my ear, then lets his fingertips trace down the side of my face.

"I know. But listen to me. Pamela is no different now than she was in high school. Besides, since when does Emma Griffin care what anyone thinks of her?"

"It's not that I care what she or any of them think of me," I insist.

"It's just you think they might be right?" he completes the thought. I stare back at him, and he shakes his head. "Do you know how often I get called out to houses because people think they hear someone trying to get in? And these are people who have never gone through anything scarier than watching a spooky Halloween marathon while eating a mummy cupcake filled with raspberry blood."

"Graphic."

"The point is, you've been through some serious shit. That's my official law enforcement jargon. Frankly, it's surprising you aren't more on edge than you are. Especially at night."

"It's not just hearing someone at the door," I tell him.

"What else happened?" he asks.

"I thought I saw my father today," I admit.

Sam's expression doesn't change. It's like the words didn't really compute, and he can't react.

"Your father?" he finally asks.

"Yes. I know it's ridiculous. It couldn't have been him. But I saw him twice today. Once before I left and then again when I was coming home after running errands." I close my eyes and shake my head. "Like

I said, my mind is slipping. That's the only explanation for it. It couldn't have been him. Of course, seeing all this doesn't help."

I gesture at the stack of papers on the table.

"What is it?" Sam asks.

"It's why I was on the phone with Eric. Remember I told you about my trip to Iowa? I requested some records. It took forever, but they finally got to my house, and Bellamy forwarded them here. Now I think I know why it took so long; there's a ton of it."

He picks up one of the papers and looks at it. "This is a deed."

"Yeah. To a house in Iowa. Not far from the Field of Dreams."

"Did you look it up?" he asks. "Find out anything about it?"

"No. But there are tax records, and my grandparents sold it to my father, who sold it when I was little. Apparently hand-me-down houses is a big thing in the family. Speaking of looking it up, I need to send scans of these to Eric." I take a picture of the deed and then reach for another document. "Look at this. It's a newspaper article about my father winning a soapbox derby competition when he was little."

"So, he grew up there. You never knew that?"

I shake my head. "No. Because he grew up here. That's the thing. He told me stories about Sherwood when he was little. There are pictures. Apparently, he grew up in two places at once. Not that the idea of somewhat ambiguous origins are all that foreign to me. But look at this. My father's actual origins are decidedly not ambiguous."

Sam takes the paper from my hand. "It's his birth certificate. He was born there."

"He was. But it's not exactly his birth certificate. That's in there, too. This is a certificate of live birth from a midwife. Whoever put this stuff together for me really dug deep. They didn't just find public records. They found whatever they could connected to my father and mother. Including this. He was born at home, not in a hospital, and the midwife filled this out as a record. It was likely filed with the court. But do you notice something strange about it?" I ask.

His eyes scan over it several times before he shakes his head. "No."

I point to a section under his name and the names of my grand-parents.

"Right here. There are two boxes. Single birth and multiple births. The 'X' isn't in either one of them completely, but part of it is in the multiples box, like when the midwife filled it out, that's where she meant to put it," I explain.

"Your father's an only child," Sam frowns.

"That's what I thought, too."

CHAPTER TWELVE

"I t's probably just a mistake. The midwife was filling it out in too much of a hurry and didn't pay enough attention to actually make sure she marked through the right box," Sam offers.

"Maybe. But it's partially in the multiples box. It's not just in a random place," I point out.

"You said his actual birth certificate is in there. What does that say?" he asks.

I sift through the papers to get the copy of my father's official birth certificate and hold it up for comparison with the midwife's form.

"It doesn't have an option for indicating single or multiple births. Not all birth certificates are the same. There are variations from state to state, and the one in Iowa doesn't have that information. It doesn't tell us anything," I tell him.

"Look at the box right next to it," Sam says, tracing his finger from the mark hovering near the multiples box to a wider box beside it. "It's supposed to be for a list of siblings. It's empty."

"I really don't know what to think. About any of this, honestly. It's a lot more than I was expecting, and I'm just trying to process it all. But it's a step. Another piece of the puzzle, even if it essentially knocks a whole bunch of the other pieces off the table." I go through the rest of the papers and photograph each of them so I can send them off to Eric. "It might tell me something about my mother's death or where my father went. Or even the man who was trying to find me when I was in Feathered Nest. I still don't know who Ron Murdock actually was or why he was there. But he led me to Iowa. Whether he realized it or not," I say.

"What do you mean, whether he realized it or not?" Sam asks.

"I still don't understand why he filled out his registration card the way he did," I explain. "He didn't put his address or even a fake address. He specifically chose a place where he couldn't possibly live but was close to the town where my father was born and where he married my mother. That can't be an accident. But it doesn't explain why he did it. If he was just trying to conceal where he lived, Murdock could have written down anything. But how would he have any idea I would read his registration card? He went out of his way to make sure he was staying at a hotel nowhere near the cabin I was staying in, even though he knew exactly where I was. He didn't want me to know where he was staying."

"Or he didn't want someone else to know," Sam suggests.

"You think he knew someone was after him?" I ask.

"It's possible. You said yourself he didn't have any luggage with him when he checked into the hotel. He obviously wasn't intending on staying in place for long. Maybe he already knew there was a chance he wasn't going to survive and leaving that address was his last resort."

"But that still begs the question. Was he there to protect me? Or to hurt me?"

"What do you hope Eric is going to find?" Sam asks.

Suddenly, I don't want to talk about this anymore. I finish taking the pictures and sweep all the papers together into a loose stack, setting the envelope down on top of it. If I keep looking at them, they're going to drive me crazy. I have to trust Eric and let him do whatever he can, so I know where to go next. But for now, I need to focus only on where I am right now.

"You didn't tell me how the investigation went," I say.

Sam stares back at me as if confused by the sudden detour in the conversation but decides not to comment on it.

"It was bleak, like any suicide is. I've always hated responding to them. Did I ever tell you the first death I had to deal with after going through the academy and joining the force was a suicide?" he asks.

I shake my head. "No. You never told me that."

He gives a tense nod. "It was only a few weeks after I joined. Everything was still fresh and enthralling. I felt invincible. Like law enforcement had never seen the likes of me." He hangs his head and lets out a short, humorless laugh. "I was positive nothing was ever going to get to me. That's not the type of cop I was going to be. I was strong and determined. Driven to see the facts and bore down to the center of every case. Then we got the call about a death at the water tower. I figured it was just going to be a transient, somebody traveling through and finally getting taken out by the bottle in his hand or the needle in his arm. There wasn't a single drop of compassion or humanity in me as we got ready to leave to respond."

"I can't imagine you without any humanity," I tell him.

"And I never could have imagined you without a sketchbook on your person, or splatters of paint on your clothes. Sometimes people lose pieces of themselves. It's whether they find them again that really makes the difference," he says.

My throat aches with the lump I swallow.

"And you found the pieces of yourself again?"

"Yeah, I did. That morning when we walked out to the water tower and found the broken body lying under it. It was a fourteen-year-old boy. He'd been lying there all night. Nobody even knew he was missing, much less that he tossed himself off the top railing. His father works all the time, and his mother was wrapped up in raising three younger siblings and working, too. They didn't think anything of it when he wanted to go out with some friends the night before. They didn't realize he never came home. We tried to find the friends he was with and couldn't find anyone. It didn't take long to figure out that it was because he didn't have any friends. The kids at school bullied him so badly no one wanted to associate with him. Eventually it drove him off that water tower. Seeing that broke me. It made me a better offi-cer, but even now, when I respond to a suicide, I think of him," Sam sighs. "I can't understand someone who does that. I can't imagine getting to that place when you genuinely don't want to live another day. Or think you don't."

"Life can put you through the grinder sometimes," I answer. "Sometimes it can seem like there isn't any point in trying to keep going because it's only going to get worse. Killing yourself doesn't feel like violence or an act of cruelty. It's mercy. Instead of trudging along through the rest of life with the days shackled to your neck, dragging along behind you, you cut the chains. You're relieved of the burden. Depression and hopelessness can be a bitch."

"I know," Sam says darkly. "But there's always more. There's always something else."

"And sometimes it's not worth the journey. Or it at the very least it, in that moment, it doesn't seem like it's worth it. The challenge is getting past that moment."

"That might have been one of the hardest parts about the investi-gation today," he says.

"What do you mean?" I ask.

"It's hard enough to deal with a suicide when it happens suddenly. Someone making a rash decision in a moment of turmoil is awful and tragic. But Everly took her time. She tormented herself for a long time. She was wearing her wedding dress and bound at the ankles. There were words written on her arms and her dress."

"Words?"

"'Disgrace. Failure. Destruction.' She took her time, which means that one flash moment of anguish for other people stretched on to probably an hour or more for Everly. That's tragedy."

"Why would she write those words on herself?" I ask.

"I think it was her way of leaving a message for the people around her. If she did have something to do with Penelope's death, those words amounted to a confession. She wasn't hiding anymore. She was offering herself up. And if she didn't, she was putting on full display what they reduced her to. In those last, black moments, she wanted her tormentors to know what they did to her. She wore her wedding dress because it was a reminder of everything she wanted and what she lost when all this happened."

"Did you have a chance to talk to anyone in the family?" I ask. "Get some insight into that theory?"

"I spoke with Michael Blair's ex and her boyfriend, and to Michael's brother. They had different reactions, to say the least."

"Why?"

"His ex, the mother of his daughter, was apparently on good terms with Everly. From all accounts, they were friendly and had no friction until Penelope's death. She is really upset and in disbelief over the whole thing. Michael's brother Daniel, on the other hand, he was cold. He didn't say it right out, but it was almost like he feels Everly killing herself was ridding the world of a problem he's glad he doesn't have to deal with anymore," Sam says.

I cringe. "Wow. And he saw the body?"

"He went in when he heard Maggie screaming. When I got there, he was still in the room with the body, messing with his phone. I had to go through his gallery to make sure he didn't take pictures. I've never seen someone that disconnected at a suicide scene before. But I guess hatred for another human will do that to you. If you think they're a waste of breath, you don't mind too much when they aren't breathing anymore."

CHAPTER THIRTEEN

FOUR AND A HALF YEARS AGO

Her hair was to her waist now. She always kept it long, liking the way people admired how thick it was and the way the blond strands fell in smooth and soft like pieces of corn silk. But never this long. It hung in a perfect braid down the center of her back, tied with a strand of pale blue leather. That's the way she always wore it. It's how he preferred it.

That's all that mattered now. What Lucas preferred, what he wanted. Women with long hair woven down their backs, tied with blue ribbon. Simple dresses and slim, delicate gold bands around their first finger. Men in slacks and buttoned shirts. The chosen with bracelets around their wrist.

But it wasn't really for Lucas. It wasn't really his preferences. That's what she was learning. This was all for the good of all people, for the future harmony they were crafting together. It wasn't always easy. Sometimes they didn't understand exactly what he wanted of them or why things had to be the way they were. When the questions came, he comforted them. They didn't need to know. They shouldn't worry themselves with trying to understand, because they never would. It was beyond their capacity. Not because they were weak, but because only he was privileged to know all the universe had hidden.

That was why he was at the head of the Society. He had been chosen at birth, cultivated in greatness, and brought through fire of the adversity to make himself into the man who would usher in the New Time. Only those deemed worthy and who proved themselves would go with him. They would understand the truly awesome power he possessed and be humbled by the wonder set before them. They would know true freedom, true joy. Gone would be crime and sadness, destruction, and betrayal.

But to get there, they must earn it. They all knew that. The New Time wasn't going to just be offered up to them. The Existence, the time of now and all who belonged to it, would fight against them. The Existence wanted everything to stay the same. They feared truth and the judgment that came with it. Purification for the New Time and the work of building it wouldn't be easy, but it would be worth it.

In the six months since arriving at The Tower, she had learned those things. They were taught to her every day, spoken to her with every breath. Around her, the people of the Society trained her. They had already dedicated their lives to their deep belief in the potential within themselves to overcome what was given to them in favor of what could be. Soon, she would be just like them. And with that would come her new name. Every word held it, hidden behind what was spoken. Every touch let it seep through their fingertips into her skin. Every look passed it from their eyes to hers. They taught her to shed The Existence to become New.

Sister Abigail. Sister Abigail. Sister Abigail.

She heard it now, where she sat in a rounded room flooded with sunlight. The curve of the walls seemed to catch it so it swirled around her, surrounding her until she couldn't deny it.

"Yes, Jeremiah?"

It was his name now. The one she used to say had disappeared, shed from her tongue, so she barely even remembered what it felt like to say it. He crossed the room to her with his hands open, and she put hers into them, letting him bring her up from her seat. He rarely touched her anymore. It would distract them both from their learning, from the purification challenges ahead of them. The time would come. Soon if they dedicated themselves enough to find it. Then all would be understood, and they would enter into the New Time as one presence. Until then, each touch was precious, and she savored them.

Now his warm, strong hands felt good on her tender joints. They were sore from the hours spent carefully copying books and poetry into thick volumes to share with others. Every piece of information anyone in The Existence read about the Society and the New Time had to be written by hand. Printing was too easy, too accessible. When they presented a document written by hand, they showed their devotion and their belief. Their blood turned to ink and bled out onto the pages through the sharpened points of their pens. Each of the women tasked with the books were more than willing to do it. This is where they were called, and it was their honor to serve in that way.

At night when her hand ached, and her eyes burned, when her body felt weakened by not eating so she could finish all that was given to her, she reminded herself why she was here. They chose her. They set her apart. It was only what was left of The Existence within her whispering questions in her ears and telling her she was tired.

"Lucas has asked for you," Jeremiah told her.

"For me?" she asked.

He smiled broadly as he nodded to her. She could see the pride in his eyes and wanted to be worthy of it. There were times when she hadn't. When she let the weakness within her take over and failed to honor him. The silence and empty coldness lasted for days. She walked through The Tower as if she didn't exist.

"There is a ceremony this afternoon. He's asked that you be a part of it."

Her heart skipped.

"I haven't finished my writing for the day," she said, turning slightly to look back at the partially filled page of the volume.

She'd been toiling over the same book for nearly a week, and she longed to finish it. But she craved Jeremiah's approval. She ached for Lucas to look at her with the kindness and admiration of that first day.

"You can work on it later. The ceremony is more important. For Lucas to choose you should be a great pleasure."

Some of the happiness had slipped from his voice, and his hands were starting to slide away from hers. She clamored to stop the descent. Gasping in a deep breath to fill her lungs with his approval, she nodded.

"It is. I just don't want to disappoint him. I will finish after the ceremony," she assured him.

The smile returned to Jeremiah's face, and he brought her out of the room, rewarding her with the linking of his fingers through hers as they made their way down the hallway. He brought her through The Tower into a section she'd never visited. Several women stood inside the tiny room, dressed in robes that brushed the stone floor. They turned to look at her as she entered, evaluating her.

"Sister Abigail," Eloise smiled, opening her arms as she stepped through the others toward her.

The other women moved to the side, parting without question. It made her feel important, like they were waiting only for her. Eloise embraced her, then looked to Jeremiah.

"Now, Jeremiah, you know you aren't allowed in the ceremony. Go on back to your work. Sister Abigail will find you later," she said.

Her heart filled with the promise. She knew what it meant. When she was given permission to find Jeremiah, it meant they were granted a short time alone together. Those few moments were droplets of honey from the comb.

As soon as he left, Eloise crossed to the other side of the room and came back with a robe draped across her arms. She held it out, expecting her to change into it without offering a place of privacy. She felt the eyes of the women on her and hurried to dress. When she was ready, they moved through a door into the next chamber, where another woman sat on a stone bench in the center of the room. She was a stranger, totally unfamiliar. But Eloise greeted her warmly before taking her by one hand.

"Sister Abigail," she said. "Come take Sister Clarissa's hand."

She walked up to the other woman, noticing her coppery hair

hung loose, nearly reaching her thighs. Taking her hand, she and Eloise led Sister Clarissa into another room. They were moving deeper into The Tower now, into a section at the heart of the structure. The room was fully round, and the ceiling rose high above them. A fireplace cut into the stone of one wall crackled, offering the room's only light. A strong, sweet smell tickled her nose and made her head dizzy. Something had been thrown into the fire, added to the burning wood to create the thick haze of incense.

The group of women following them stayed huddled behind them as she followed Eloise's lead to guide Sister Clarissa up onto a platform in the center of the room. Up until now, there had been no sign of Lucas. She was tempted to ask about him. After all, Jeremiah said he was the one who asked for her. But she kept quiet. She didn't want to lose her privilege or look helpless.

Once on the platform, they lowered Sister Clarissa's hands, and Eloise started releasing the buttons on the back of her dress. Eloise glanced down at the redheaded woman's wrists as if to indicate the buttons there, and she reached for them, unbuttoning them though she didn't understand why. After a few minutes, the firelight danced on pale bare skin, and she tried not to show her discomfort at the woman standing there naked in front of her. As Eloise helped Sister Clarissa onto a raised bed in the middle of the platform, the rest of the women gathered around them. Eloise stood at Sister Clarissa's head, resting her hands on her hair.

"Sister Abigail," she said, nodding her head toward the other woman's feet.

She took her place there, taking hold of Sister Clarissa's ankles the way Eloise held her head. Eloise drew in a breath.

"Today we celebrate Sister Clarissa's first phase of purification and her acceptance into the Circle of Light," she said.

A door to the side she hadn't noticed slid open, and a cloaked figure entered. As she got closer, she recognized the figure as Ruth, Lucas's wife. She said nothing as she walked over to the fireplace and took hold of a long metal pole. She pulled it out of the flames, and with it came a small metal branding iron, glowing red. The women parted as she climbed up onto the platform.

She saw Sister Clarissa's eyes close and felt her body shake beneath her hands. Long, pale fingers grasped at the sides of the bed beneath her, desperate for something to hold onto. As Ruth got closer, Eloise's hold on Sister Clarissa's head tightened, and she followed suit with Sister Clarissa's ankles.

The sweet smell of the fire had meaning now. She held tight to thrashing ankles as the skin on Sister Clarissa's waist melted away. Tears stung her eyes, but shock kept them from sliding down her cheeks. Sister Clarissa bit down into her bottom lip, drawing blood to hold back her scream. It dragged on, the seconds longer and longer. Finally, Ruth pulled away the iron. She rested a kiss to the center of Sister Clarissa's forehead, returned the iron to the fireplace, and walked out of the room.

Eloise took up a pitcher of water from a small table sitting to the side of the table and poured it over Sister Clarissa. Her back arched as her skin cooled, and a sob broke through her mangled lips. But when she opened her eyes, she looked right at Eloise.

"Thank you," she whispered.

The others left in silence. Eloise walked up to her and offered her hands. She took them and let the other woman hold them tightly.

"Sister Abigail, you are blessed to have been here and witnessed this glorious moment," Eloise said with a warm smile. "Sister Clarissa has been welcomed into the Circle of Light. She will be cherished by Lucas and offered a treasured place in the New Time." Eloise stroked her face. "We all have our calling. You will come to yours. Lucas favors you."

CHAPTER FOURTEEN

NOW

Sam felt left out after missing the cinnamon rolls at game night, so before he left last night, I promised to make some for him and have them ready before he went into the station this morning. I made the dough and left them to rise in the refrigerator, then popped them in the oven while I took my morning shower. I stepped out into house filled with the glorious smell of cinnamon and sugar all wrapped up in tender yeast dough. It's one of the great joys of life. No one should have to grow old without a few mornings that smell like this.

Sam lets out a sigh of appreciation as he steps into the house, carrying a bag of my favorite coffee beans from the roaster in town. I reach up into the cabinet for my bean grinder, and he wraps his arms around my waist from behind, nuzzling his face into the curve of my neck.

"Smells amazing," he says.

"Me or the cinnamon rolls?" I ask.

"Both," he says and kisses my shoulder.

I pour some of the coffee beans into the grinder and blitz them, then pour them into the coffee maker.

"The rolls will be ready in just a couple of minutes," I tell him. "The icing is already ready."

"Did you make extra?" he asks.

"Would I ever do anything but?"

He takes a spoon out of the drawer and perches at the table as I pour coffee. Pulling the bowl of cream cheese frosting close to him, he dips the spoon in and samples it. I shake my head and laugh at him. The man has no control.

"You never told me why the management company wanted you to come up there yesterday," he starts.

I put the cream back in the refrigerator and slide a cup of the fragrant coffee toward him.

"Oh. So, it turns out when Dad decided to turn over the house to the management company to be rented out, there was still some stuff in the attic and the storage shed. They called him and told him it was there, but instead of coming to get it, he asked them to put it in the storage unit and just pay for it until he came back. Obviously, he never did. The other night, somebody tried to break into it. They didn't get all the way in, but they banged the living hell out of the lock." I take a sip of my coffee. "Didn't you know about it already? I figured you would have heard from the manager of the storage unit."

He shook his head. "I didn't hear anything about it. He didn't make a report."

"That's interesting. I wonder why he didn't."

"Didn't want the hassle or the bad look of an officer roaming around his property. Makes it look like it's not secure."

"Which it's not. The security cameras on the unit buildings are fakes," I tell him.

"Another reason he doesn't want to tell us. He knows he'll get poked fun at for cheapening out with toy security cameras," Sam nods. "What was in the unit?"

"A chair and a stack of boxes. I was kind of hoping for a treasure chest or scary mannequin or something," I say.

"Were you actually hoping for a scary mannequin?" he raises an eyebrow.

"No. But those TV shows are very misleading."

I go to the oven to take out the rolls.

"Those TV shows are very scripted with people who buy stuff just to stock the supposedly abandoned units," he points out.

I sigh as I put the pan down on a pair of trivets on the table.

"What has happened to reality TV? Gone are the days of girls slinging their shirts off for no apparent reason and fractured marriages turning to parking lot brawls and storming of various places of business," I tease.

"Also all scripted," he chuckles, lifting the bowl to pour the icing over the hot rolls.

"What is the world coming to? I've been so misled." I tear off a piece of one of the cinnamon rolls. The molten brown sugar stings on my fingers, but it's worth it. "I didn't get a chance to go through the boxes. I was already running late, so I only looked through the Christmas decorations in the first one. I'm planning on going back to look through them."

"Do you want to come up to the station with me? I'll take you up there during my lunch break."

I give him a questioning look. "You want me to come up to the station and sit there while you work just so you can bring me up to the storage unit during lunch?" I ask.

"I might be a bit curious, too. I also want to have a word with the manager about his responsibility to inform the department of incidents. Having you there will also give me a good reason to not work through lunch."

He leans across the table to kiss me.

"Nothing says romance like sitting in the waiting room of a police station reading old magazines. But for you, I'll find out about the breakup of the century again. What's on your schedule today?" I ask.

"More paperwork about Everly Zara. Still trying to hunt down Michael Blair as well."

"You know, I've been thinking about what you told me about the suicide," I say, getting up and going to the utensil canister on the counter for a pair of metal tongs to dish out the rolls. "It's not really sitting right with me."

"What do you mean?" he asks, getting plates from the cabinet and sitting back down.

"From what I remember about her, they were very happy before the little girl died. After that, she fought hard against the allegations and was very outspoken about wanting to clear her name and get her life back together. She never took her wedding ring off and talked about her future with Michael. She never once hinted she thought her relationship was really over or that she would be legally blamed for Penelope's death."

"You're right. She was completely adamant she didn't do anything to Penelope and that her death was an accident. The only thing she would ever say was she should have watched her more closely in those few moments," Sam nods. "Apparently she was running around on the marble floor in her socks. Everly always said the baby liked to run around, and she would tell her that she could fall, but that night she started running and slipped."

"Exactly. So, what's the motivation behind such a dramatic suicide? You pointed out it wasn't a moment of passion. She didn't get so distraught she all of a sudden decided to throw herself off the balcony or take an overdose. This looked like something she thought out and prepared for."

"So?" he asks, filling his mouth with a huge bite of cinnamon roll.

"Why would she swing so drastically? Nothing happened that would make her suddenly go from determined to clear her name and move forward with her life to making a dramatic statement with a ritualistic suicide."

"Are you saying you think she didn't kill herself?"

"I'm just wondering what else led to the conclusion she did," I tell him.

"The scene suggested she stood on the footboard of the bed, attached the rope to the ceiling fan, and jumped. She had no defensive wounds on her hands or signs of assault of any kind. The house was locked up from the inside. All doors and windows. Maggie, the housekeeper who found her, used her key to get inside. The security cameras that cover the entire perimeter of the house are motion activated. Any movement makes them turn on and record for several minutes. None were tripped at any point before Maggie showed up. I know it doesn't make a lot of sense, but the evidence points to suicide."

I nod. "Alright."

"Maybe all that confidence was just for show. She thought if she acted like everything was fine, it would bring Michael back to her and stop the investigation into Penelope's death. But when it didn't look like that was going to happen, she couldn't take it anymore. Now we just help everyone around her pick up the pieces and move on."

I have to admit it's a solid theory. But still, something doesn't sit right with me.

CHAPTER FIFTEEN

We get to the police station, and I take my place in the waiting room. I could probably go back to his office with him, but it wouldn't be good form. Considering the professional capacity that brought me back to Sherwood to work with Sam, I don't want to muddy the waters. Besides, he's never been good at concentrating when I'm nearby. The few times I attempted to help him study for a test and upcoming projects are testament to that. Something about me just being in the same room with him seems to keep his brain from being able to follow a straight path. He'll do what he needs to do eventually, but it can be a winding road to get there. This doesn't come into play when he's deep in the mire of an intense investigation. But he already said this morning is set aside for paperwork, and that never thrills him.

He'll come out during breaks, and I'll end up in conversation with the other officers. I may wander around in the small garden in the back of the building. It's the same pattern I follow any time I come into the station with Sam. I'm not good at not doing anything. Even those days when I tell myself I just want to be lazy; it doesn't work out for me. I can grow roots and be a couch potato with the best of them after a long day, but when morning hits, I need to be doing something.

That's been one of the hardest parts of taking this break from the Bureau. Long days stretched out in front of me without work to fill them have driven me to bake, and I've been getting dangerously close to starting the unthinkable pastime of crafting.

So I fill the time by occasionally popping by the station or tagging along. It also ensures I'm in on the good gossip from around town. The petty crimes. The drunken fights. Apparently, the only thing I've missed is the talk of my mind slipping away into the ether. It's a trade-off.

But there isn't going to be any gossiping this morning. I don't even get a chance to flip through a magazine. Instead, the sound of shouting brings me to my feet and out to the main portion of the lobby. The station is designed to isolate the waiting room away from the rest of the station. The front desk acts as sentry in front of the door to the back. It seems like a nice way to protect the privacy of those waiting for visits or to pick up loved ones getting sprung from their time behind bars. It's a nice thought, but I know it's much more likely a safety measure. Rather than keeping those people from prying eyes, it keeps them from flying bullets and angry intruders.

Which is what sounds like is happening now. Instinct brings me to my feet, and I run toward the sound of people shouting in the lobby. When I get there, I find two officers trying to hold back a man and woman trying to force their way into the back of the station. The woman looks familiar. It only takes me a second to realize it's Payton, Michael Blair's ex-girlfriend and the mother of his child.

"You need to calm down," Dennis Long, a tall, dark-haired officer is saying, holding up a hand to push Payton back.

"Let us through," she insists.

"Back up," the other officer, a woman named Savanna, commands.

"We need to talk to Sheriff Johnson," the man I assume is Payton's boyfriend says, pressing his chest toward the officer like he's hoping it will force her out of the way.

"What's going on here?" I ask.

"You're Emma Griffin," Payton says.

I nod as I approach her.

"Yes," I say, keeping my voice calm.

In situations like this, the fastest way to deescalate a person is to keep your voice calm and steady. It's often an instinct to match the volume and intensity of the person's voice. But that would only push them further. Instead, I force their attention and give them time to breathe by speaking quietly and slowly. It seems to have some of an effect on Payton now. She turns away from the officers.

"You help Sheriff Johnson with cases sometimes," she says.

"I helped him with a case earlier this year." Not confirming, not denying.

"Tell them I need to talk to him. You can convince them," she almost pleads.

"Why don't you tell me what's going on?" I ask.

"We need to talk to the sheriff about the investigation into my daughter's death," she says. "Please."

"Let me bring you to the waiting room. I'll go back and find the sheriff and have him come out to talk to you," I offer.

She hesitates, then flashes a look over at her boyfriend. He nods. I guide them in front of me so I can keep an eye on their movements. The anger and anxiety radiate off of them. I know from experience, people tend to be routine and predictable until the moment they aren't. That moment can mean disaster. They come with me to the waiting room without incident, and I settle them into place, making sure Dennis and Savannah are posted at the doorway between the waiting room and the hallway.

Rushing back to the lobby, I ask the woman behind the desk to call Sam for me. She nods, fear etched on her face. Seconds later, he appears at the door.

"Missing me already?" he asks with a teasing smile.

"No," I say. "But somebody is."

The smile on his face disappears, and his eyes narrow.

"What do you mean?"

"Payton is in the waiting room," I tell him. "She and some guy stormed in here, demanding to see you. They're angry and say they need to talk about your investigation into Penelope's death."

He gives an understanding nod as he processes the situation.

"That would be her boyfriend, Ian. Where are they?" he asks.

"I brought them back to the waiting area."

We immediately head down the hall and find Payton up, pacing through the rows of padded blue chairs. Ian stands close to the doorway; his arms crossed over his chest as he stares past the officers toward us. As soon as she notices Sam, Payton rushes forward.

"How could you? How could you?" she demands.

"Payton, you need to calm down and tell me what's going on," he starts.

"You know damn well what's going on," Ian cuts in, stepping forward.

"You aren't investigating Penelope's death anymore," Payton says.

Sam draws in a breath and lets it out slowly. "Let's go to my office." He eyes me. "Emma, this is Payton Jennings and Ian Mills. This is Emma Griffin. Do you mind if she sits in?"

"No. Maybe she'll be able to talk some sense into you," Payton says.

Tears sparkling in her eyes make their emerald color brighter.

We go to Sam's office. He shuts the door before sitting down and leaning toward them.

"I wish I had been the one to tell you about the change," he says.

"Well, you weren't. We had to hear it from some pissant cop crawling around taking pictures at Blair's house," Ian snaps.

"That shouldn't have happened, and I apologize. I wanted to call you in and discuss it with you," Sam says.

"You shouldn't have to discuss anything with us. How could you stop the investigation?" Payton asks.

"I assure you; the case has not stopped. Unfortunately, with Everly's death, there is no case to investigate at this time."

"No case? Penelope is still dead," Ian spits.

"I know. And I am still so sorry for your loss. But the case didn't revolve around whether her death occurred, but if Ms. Zara had anything to do with it. The purpose of the investigation was to determine if there were any grounds for criminal charges to be brought up against her. With her no longer alive, there is no one to charge. Therefore, this investigation can't currently continue until we explore the connections between Penelope's and Ms. Zara's deaths," Sam explains carefully.

"So, that's it? Just like that?" Payton asks. "My daughter is dead. She was two years old, and now she's gone."

"I know that."

"But it doesn't mean anything now? It mattered, but now it doesn't anymore?" Ian asks.

"It's not that it doesn't matter. Of course it matters. Penelope's death is a tragedy, no matter what led to it. The point is, continuing to pursue the investigation without broader context wouldn't be a good use of time, energy, or resources. And these are resources we need to continue investigating both cases to find their connections. But, frankly, without Everly to tell us exactly what happened that night, there is little chance of knowing what happened that night. I assure you; I'm doing everything I can to try to do this investigation the right way. And that means that right now, for the current moment, there is nothing directly in Penelope's case we even have to investigate. For the time being, it might be best for everyone involved to try to move forward."

Payton sags in her chair. After a long pause, she scoffs and shakes her head.

"Move forward. Just that simple. Next month on Halloween, when all the other children are trick-or-treating, my daughter will still be dead. On Thanksgiving, when she should be making turkeys out of the outline of her hand, she will be dead. On Christmas, when she should be trying to stay up to watch for Santa, she will be dead. And on New Year's Eve, when everybody else is kissing and celebrating a fresh year ahead of them, I will be looking at the first year that my daughter isn't alive in since she was born."

She stands up and stares into Sam's face, venom coating every word.

"But sure, Sherriff. It will be easy to just move on."

CHAPTER SIXTEEN

"What happened?" I ask twenty minutes later as I watch a drop of condensation roll down my water glass.

"With what?" Sam asks.

"With Penelope," I say, raising my eyes up to him.

"I told you, no one is sure," he says. "Everly said she fell while she was running around playing, but there seems to be some evidence of multiple traumas to the head, like she was dropped or slammed on the floor."

I shake my head.

"That's not what I mean. I mean, what happened with her parents? Most of the time, the mother gets custody, right? Especially with a child as young as Penelope. Even when the father is far wealthier and has more resources, as long as the mother isn't dangerous or some sort of addict, she gets the baby. Is that what happened? Was Payton an addict?" I ask.

"No," Sam says.

"Then what? She seems devastated. What I just witnessed in there was heartbreaking. Why didn't Penelope live with her?" I ask.

"Because she didn't want her to," a voice says from beside the table.

I look up, startled by the flat, almost emotionless answer. A man with inky eyes and a drawn, chiseled face stares down at us. I recognize him from the news coverage of Penelope's death and then Everly's. It's Michael Blair.

"Michael," Sam says. "We've been trying to get in touch with you."

"I know," he says. "I've been disconnected. I went to the station to talk to you, but they said you were here. I hope you don't mind."

"Of course not," Sam says.

He slides out of his side of the booth and comes over to join me so Michael can sit across from us. There's a strange moment of expectation, both sides of the table waiting for the other one to say something and guide the conversation. I try to understand the emotion on his face and the way he holds his body. What a person doesn't say is often far more powerful than what they do. But I can't read him. He holds himself steady, firm and in place like nothing affects him. His expression hasn't changed.

"Payton and I were never a serious relationship. She was a lot of fun, and we enjoyed being together, but neither one of us was confused about what we were. There were no delusions of a passionate love connection or a future together. That didn't change when she found out she was pregnant. She wasn't sleeping with anyone else, so I knew the baby was mine. I was excited. Being a father was always something I envisioned, and it didn't really matter to me what the circumstances were. Some people might have wanted me to, but I didn't buy into the idea that it would have somehow been better if he was born to a married couple. That wasn't something Payton or I wanted. We didn't mind being together. We enjoyed each other, and our relationship worked. For a time. But she didn't want to be a mother."

"She didn't want Penelope?" I ask.

"That's a heavily loaded question. But it's one nobody ever thinks twice about asking. The reality is, no. She didn't want her. She never imagined herself having children and was beyond shocked when it happened. For a long time, she was under the impression she was incapable of having children. Not that we weren't still careful. But she happened anyway."

A distant light comes in his eyes, rising at the same time as pain. He ran his fingers back through his dark blond hair, making it stand out for a brief moment before it fell back into place.

"She was a miracle. That doesn't mean her thoughts about having children suddenly changed. I think it's a really popular notion that some people just don't know they want children until they have one. I don't think that's always the truth. I think it's much more likely that people who don't want children find themselves in circumstances where they have them, and their only way to cope with it is to convince everyone around them they are suddenly deliriously happy, that they saw the light and their whole lives fell into place. It's not only dishonest; it's damaging."

"Damaging?" I frown.

"When people say that, they have no idea who they're talking to. The person who hears it might still be holding onto feelings of hesitation or fear. They might not be excited or feel like they could possibly handle having a child. Hearing that can just leave them feeling more broken and alone. No one should feel that way, and no child should be raised by someone who felt that way. So, did Payton want Penelope? No. She didn't. But did she love her? Absolutely."

The three of us sit in awkward silence for about a minute too long. What could I even say to that?

"How long were you together after she was born?" I finally manage to get out.

"Not long. Payton had her own life to live, and I had mine. It wasn't hard to come up with a plan for how we were going to raise the baby. I wanted her with me, and I could afford to give her everything I possibly could in life. She would have visitation and come to see her whenever she wanted to. It was exactly right. For all of us. There were legal papers, but they didn't require hours in court or a judge making proclamations. We sat in my living room with my attorney. It was smooth and easy. And it stayed smooth and easy. She saw Penelope all the time, and there was never any discomfort or difficulty between us. We always got along. She even got along really well with..."

His voice cuts off in a painful choke, and he looks down at his hands folded on the table. The waitress comes by with our food and lowers plates in front of us. She looks at Michael with expectation, but he shakes his head, and she walks away.

"Look, Michael," Sam starts. "I know this is a horrible time for you, and I am so sorry to have to do this, but I'm going to need to talk to you about a few things. Can we set up a time for you to come by my office?"

"Let's do it now," he says.

"We don't have to," Sam says. "I can imagine this is not something you really want to talk about here in the diner."

"I don't want to talk about it at all. I don't want to have to talk about it. I want to go home to my wife and my daughter. But it's never going to happen again. Nothing is going to make this conversation comfortable. If I have to have it, I'd rather get it over with."

Sam nods.

"It's my understanding you haven't gone back to your house since the night Penelope was injured. Is that true?" he asks.

"Yes. I went to the hospital and stayed with her," Michael answers.

"And after she died?" Sam asks.

He does it in the straightforward, matter-of-fact way that is the only way to manage that type of question. Trying to be too gentle or tender could stir up difficult emotions. It's better to come at it clearly.

"For reasons you can probably understand, I didn't much want to go back to the house. Instead, I went to one of my other properties," Michael answers.

"What other property?" Sam asks.

"A mountain cabin. It's somewhat remote, a few hours' drive from here. It gives me the quiet I need to think."

"And you've been there ever since?"

"Yes. I went up there the night Penelope died and haven't come back until today. There's no television in the cabin, and I don't listen to the radio. Cell service is spotty at best, but I tend to turn my phone off when I'm up there, anyway. Being tethered to my regular life through technology kind of defeats the purpose of a respite. I didn't hear about Everly until very early this morning when my brother finally got ahold of me. You can imagine how startling it was to listen to news reports on my way here. I would think the media would be tasteful enough to wait until I was properly notified before splashing the story all over," Michael tells us.

"I'm sorry you had to hear those reports, and I understand your frustration with how it is being handled. Unfortunately, the media only really feels obligated to wait until the next of kin is notified. Since we were able to find Everly's parents for notification, they consider that enough," Sam explains.

Michael nods, his lips pursed together as he thinks through the implications.

"Good enough," he says bitterly. "I guess they would say that. I am her next of kin, so they should have waited to notify me. But since they weren't able to get in touch with me as soon as they wanted to, they just moved on to the next names on the list. It's just that simple. Nothing could possibly go wrong with that.

"How did you feel about your ongoing relationship with her?" Sam asks.

"What do you mean?"

"With the questions concerning the death of your daughter and you not coming home to stand by her, it looks like you were considering ending the relationship," I say. "Not that anyone would blame you."

"I wasn't planning on ending my relationship with Everly. If anything, I hadn't come to a solid decision yet. But I was far from being sure I didn't want her in my life anymore. I loved her. More than I've ever loved anyone. More than I ever knew was possible to love someone. It didn't take long after I met her to know she was who I wanted to spend my life with. I couldn't imagine going through the most painful thing I ever experienced, the loss of my daughter, without her. At the same time, I couldn't face her."

"Do you think she hurt Penelope?" Sam asks.

He's following a delicate balance between discussing Everly's suicide and venturing into the investigation he already decided to put on the back burner.

"No," Michael says. "Everly adored Penelope, and she adored her. They were everything to each other. She could never hurt her."

"Then why haven't you spoken up for her?" I ask.

He shakes his head. "I don't know. I should have."

"Just one more thing and I'll let you go," Sam says. "Did she ever express anything to you about wanting to hurt herself?"

"No. I didn't hear from her at all after that night. She didn't try to get in touch with me. Not even right before she did it. I guess I was the last thing on her mind," he says.

I shake my head.

"I think you were the only thing on it."

CHAPTER SEVENTEEN

HIM

People always think keys are necessary to get into houses without calling attention. He knew that wasn't the case. They make things easier. It's simpler and less time-consuming to just be able to walk up to a door and put a key in. Over the years, it became second nature to him to find ways of getting copies of people's keys. When he wanted access to their home or their business, he'd simply use one of these methods to get his hands on their keys and create his own copies. Instantly their world was open to him. Once he knew their patterns and schedules and was able to find and deactivate pesky features like security cameras and alarms, he could come and go as he pleased.

It wasn't so simple with Emma. The police coverage of her other house was dwindling. After not seeing anything suspicious or having anything to report back to her, it seemed less and less pressing to have them around at all times. Soon it would only be once or twice a day that they circled around and checked. Then a few times a week. Then one day, they just wouldn't return at all. But that's not what he was concerned about right then. Now his focus was on the house in Sherwood. He hadn't been able to get access to her keys. She always kept them far too close and didn't do any of the things he relied on when wanting to slip a keyring away.

It didn't stop him. Again, keys make things easier. But they aren't necessary. There are many other ways to get inside somewhere without the luxury of the key. Fortunately, the almost dizzying peace and quiet of the neighborhood was on his side. There were no neighbors to the back, and tall Ivy-covered privacy fences to either side kept the backyard tastefully isolated. Even if there were people around to notice him there and be suspicious of his presence, they wouldn't see him when he got to the back door. He would be hidden from view, able to take his time and leave no trace.

This time he had to be sure Emma wasn't home. He made such a stupid mistake the night before. When he saw how dark the house was, he was positive she wasn't there. Her car was sitting in the driveway, but that meant little. She spent almost as much time in the Sheriff's car as she did her own. Seeing the back-porch light on only made him feel more confident. She always turned the light over the back-door on in the evening. She always had. No matter where she was living, if there was a light to be turned on, it didn't stay dark after the sun went down.

But that time, she did. When he got into the backyard, he paused only long enough to slide the brick out of place on the side of the porch. It's not that he really thought a key would still be there, or that even if there was it would still work in the lock. It was more to check to make sure the brick was still loose. If anyone ever fixed that brick and secured it fully into place, the house would lose more of what it once was. After slipping the brick back into place, he got to the door, reassured and comforted by the darkness, and went to work on the lock. If he was careful and didn't let himself get too excited, he could get through the lock without breaking it or leaving marks.

That was the most difficult part. Holding back his excitement. It buzzed inside him, making his blood feel effervescent, and his thoughts bubble and pop around the edges. Getting inside here was even more than her other house. Even more... what? He couldn't really finish the sentence. Even more thrilling. Even more personal. Just, more.

What amounted to an alarm system on the house was nothing more than a mechanical scream that went off when a door opened. It could be silenced with just the turn of a stick key in the metal panel on the wall. Experience watching her go into the house enough times told him she rarely activated the system when she wasn't going to be in the house. It was a fairly worthless sound, not connected to anything or anyone, and he could assume by the creative profanities she flung when it went off that she hated the sound.

He wasn't going to be the way he was the night before. Too eager. He didn't pay enough attention and nearly got himself caught first by her, then by the sheriff arriving at the front door. Today he knew she was gone. He watched her ride away in the sheriff's car, and she hadn't come back. He had the lock, and the house it offered up to him, all to himself.

His tools rarely failed him, and they didn't now. The lock opened easily. Almost too easily. Hopefully she would consider replacing the locks on that door. He didn't want to think of Emma being in any danger when she was home.

As soon as the lock popped open, he slipped his tools back in his pack and stood to slip inside. He walked through years to step into that kitchen. The smell of cinnamon and yeast dough lingered in the air, and it could have been hanging there since the last time he smelled it. Walking further into the house, he watched as his mind superimposed images of the past with what he saw now. So much had changed. Much of it was barely recognizable. But there were details that couldn't be altered. No matter how long between visits. No matter what family took over for their temporary time in the house. Some things about it could never be different.

His feet easily followed the path they walked many times before to bring him to the door to the attic. Unlike many houses, there was no trapdoor or dangling string to reveal folding stairs and an unstable railing. A door that looked like it could lead to any bedroom opened up to a sturdy wooden staircase that led into the attic. It was large by the standards of the house, finished with a stable floor and walls rather than the exposed beams and insulation of most attics.

He climbed the stairs but found nothing. He hoped Emma would have brought the contents of the storage unit back to the house and tucked them away up here. It would be easier for him to go through, but there was nothing there. Giving a last fleeting look to the open space, he climbed back down the steps and roamed the rest of the house. He should have been more cautious. Emma could get back home any minute with the sheriff in tow, and he should have searched out what he wanted and left.

But he was drawn into the house, captivated by the damage of daily life buffed out of the floors, the layers of paint sealing time into the walls, the pictures no longer hanging there. He moved along the hallway slowly, taking it in. He searched through her room, running his fingers along the edge of her dresser and breathing in the smell of her clinging to her bedding.

By the time he made it into the living room, he hadn't found anything that looked like it came from the storage unit. She must have left it all there. It was frustrating, but just before he walked back out of the house, he noticed something sitting on the coffee table. A manila envelope sitting on a stack of papers, with a familiar return address. Moving the envelope aside, he sifted through the papers. A smile curled his lips.

"What are you up to, Emma?" he whispered.

Some of his humor faded when he found the certificate of live birth from the midwife. He stared at it for several long seconds before folding it in half, slipping it into his jacket, and rushing away.

CHAPTER EIGHTEEN

"So, what did you think?" Sam asks after Michael leaves.

"What do you mean?"

"About him. What do you think about him? I know you well enough to know you formed an opinion."

I pop the rest of a french fry into my mouth and take the opportunity of chewing to glare across the table at him.

"I feel like I should be offended right now," I tell him.

"Yet you're not," he points out. "Because you know it's true as much as I do. I saw you watching him from the moment he sat down with us. You weren't just having a conversation with him. You were evaluating him. So, tell me. What's the verdict? What did you think about him?"

"I don't know, I admit. He's so... even. I don't really know how else to describe it."

"Emotionless?" Sam asks.

"No. Not emotionless. He definitely showed something. But it was subdued like he has a lot of practice tightly controlling everything he thinks and feels and shows."

"Someone as wealthy and powerful as him probably does," Sam nods. "He spends his entire life interacting with other people who all have expectations of him. His money isn't old. Not that his family was ever wanting for much, but Michael Blair created Michael Blair. Everybody knows that and has very strong opinions on what that means and what it should look like."

"I guess that explains why his brother lives in the in-law suite rather than his own place," I muse. "Riding his brother's coattails a bit?"

"Michael and Daniel have always been close. Daniel was adopted when Michael was about eight, and they have been a unit since. Ever since Michael took his inheritance and started nurturing it into a business empire, he made sure to bring his brother along with him. He's kept him in a good job, taken care of him."

"And the way Daniel thanks him is to openly hate his brother's wife?" I ask. "That doesn't sound particularly loving to me."

"Daniel has always wanted to take care of Michael the way he's taking care of him. He doesn't do it in the same way; he always keeps an eye out for him. He watches over him and wants what's best for him. That's always been screening clients and managing aspects of the business so Michael could concentrate on the parts of that he was passionate about. But when he met Everly, things changed. To hear it from Daniel, he immediately pegged her as nothing but a gold digger. She wanted the type of life Michael could give her because it's not something that she ever could have had any other way.

In a way, I think he felt he knew better because he didn't come from the same privilege as Michael. Like I said, they weren't exorbitantly wealthy or anything, but the Blair family was certainly up there in the top fringe of the middle class. If there really is such a thing as the upper-middle class, that's them. Even though Daniel was very young when he was adopted, he has made a few statements about remembering what life was like before he was with the Blairs. It was rough, and it affected him. Maybe when he looked at Everly, he thought he saw someone coming from modest means who wanted to find the easy way to the good life."

"How did he know about her family?" I ask.

"Everly didn't lie about where she came from or her family. Some

THE GIRL IN THE MANOR

women try to hide their pasts or come up with personas to slip into society and snag a wealthy man. But not her. She didn't mind talking about her parents, or that she was from an immigrant family. She came from meager beginnings and was working hard to find her way in life. Apparently, she didn't really have much of an option but to tell him that. They met in a restaurant, but she was the waitress, not another patron."

"Did he have this kind of problem with Payton?"

"Not that anybody's mentioned. He didn't express any distaste toward her, either. According to him, they all got along," Sam shrugs.

"That doesn't make any sense. Payton didn't come from money and isn't exactly the kind of woman I would think of as sophisticated. Nothing against her personally, of course, I'm just not going to eagerly anticipate seeing her name in the society pages. And she had Michael's baby," I point out.

"Who Daniel absolutely adored. He didn't come right out and talk about it, but I think he had the same type of opinion about their relationship as Michael and Payton did. He didn't see anything serious or lasting between them. It didn't really matter who she was as long as she made him happy for the time and then went along her way. That was the difference with Everly. She caught Michael's attention in a completely different way. She was young and beautiful, bold and vivacious, but also playful and sweet. She was everything Michael ever wanted in a wife and a mother figure for Penelope. She had her biological mother, of course, and she was very involved. But Michael saw Everly being in the home with them and making a huge difference in both their lives. In Daniel's mind, it was all an act on her part. She saw his vulnerability as a single father and took advantage of it to position herself to rake in a continuous stream of money for as long as their marriage lasted."

"You sound like you agree with him," I note.

Sam takes a sip of his drink and shakes his head as he swallows.

"No. It's not that I agree with him. I can just see his perspective. I've dealt with plenty of men scorned by pretty women who manipulate their way into the men's lives, drain them, then leave them broke and tattered. And I've known the family and friends around those men who always say they wish they'd known the type of person the woman was, or they would have said something if they did have suspicions. There's always regret not warning the person earlier or trying to convince them to leave the woman alone. With Daniel, he wasn't willing to have that regret if he could help it. He wanted to make sure his brother knew he didn't think Everly was good enough for him. He thought she was just warming up for a life as a pampered trophy wife. He's made a few statements suggesting he thinks that's why Everly killed Penelope. Pretending to fawn all over him was getting to her, and she didn't want anyone standing in the way of her time with Michael."

"So, he didn't like Everly because he didn't think she was good enough to be in their family, and because his brother actually found someone he wanted to marry? And he blamed her for a child's death because he thought she was just trying to get rid of him so she could have Michael and his money all to herself?"

"That's what I get out of it," Sam says.

"That's lovely," I mutter, wiping my fingers on a napkin and tossing it onto the table. "Here's the thing. We all want to think we know exactly how someone should react in any given situation. We want to pretend we have it all figured out, and if someone is acting a different way, that we know for sure what's going on in their mind. That's not the case. Nobody ever knows how they are actually going to react to something happening until it happens to them. Until they are standing in that situation and staring down the barrel at it, they don't know what they would do. And neither does anyone else. You can tell a lot about someone from their emotions and how they act. But you can also tell nothing at all."

"Speaking of deep hidden secrets and lovely mysteries unfolding, what do you say we head over to the storage unit?" Sam asks.

"Wow. You truly are working on becoming a master of conversation segues, aren't you?" I say flatly.

"I dream big. Come on. Eventually they're going to want me back at the station. but we're just a couple of minutes away from the storage unit, so we might as well swing by."

He pays for lunch, and we make our way to the storage unit. Part of me expects to see more damage done to the door, or even the new lock snapped off. Instead, it looks like no one has bothered the area since I was here yesterday. I glance over at the woods. I don't feel the same strange awareness this time. Climbing out of the car, I gesture to the door to the storage unit.

"This is it," I tell him. I walk up to the door and release the firm new lock. The door opens, and I pat the top of the first plastic tote. "This is the one I went through yesterday. It's a bunch of Christmas decorations I don't recognize. None of them seemed massively old. I mean, a few of them have some years on them, but I wouldn't quite make the leap to these being precious heirloom pieces."

"You don't remember any of them?" he asks.

"No. None of them look familiar. I don't know why they kept it."

Moving the box of Christmas decorations to the side, I pry open the next box. It doesn't seem to be much more than clothes. At the very bottom of the box is a pair of shoes. They look familiar, but I can't quite place them, and that makes me squirm slightly. I open the third box, and my heart jumps a little.

"What is it? What did you find?" Sam asks.

"Pictures," I tell him. "This whole tote is full of pictures. Look, it's my grandparents when they were younger."

"It looks like a wedding," Sam says, taking the picture and looking down at my grandmother and grandfather gazing at each other as they danced in each other's arms. "There are people in the background, watching them."

He shows me the picture again.

"They got married when they were much younger than this. Here," I point to the picture, "this is my father, see? This must be when they renewed their vows. My grandmother told me about that. Apparently, I was there. I was very little, but I was there."

I pick up a handful of other pictures and start flipping through them. Sam stares into the box with a hint of awe.

"There could be thousands of pictures in there. That's incredible," he says.

I barely hear him. I force myself to swallow and feel like the rock in my throat sinks down, then rises right back up.

"I only need this one," I manage to say, staring down at the picture in my hand. The rest slip out, some sliding back into the tote while others fall from the side of the box and ended up on the floor.

"What is it?" he asks.

I touch my fingertips to the picture.

"My mother."

CHAPTER NINETEEN

I always thought my mother was the most beautiful woman in the world. I never had the opportunity to see her dance in Russia. There aren't any video recordings, only pictures of her on the stage. In her pristine costumes, her elegance and poise were breathtaking. She commanded the attention of every single person in that room. It's why she was celebrated and loved. But the world of ballet wasn't enough to hold her. It wasn't deep in her heart. When an injury took her off stage, she had a choice. She could have fought her way back, by pushing her body to recover, and demanding to take her spot again. If she hadn't been able to perform at the same level, she could have become an instructor and led her own company.

But that wasn't her dream. She wanted so much more than a life that was chosen for her in Russia. She dreamed of coming to the United States and crafting her own reality, her own future. She wanted love and a family. It took incredible courage for her to walk away from the security of the role selected for her when she was still so young, from the only world she had ever really known. It took even more to pack up what she could bring with her and come to a completely new world, a new country where she knew no one and had to start completely over.

It doesn't matter that I never got to see her dance. I can imagine it in my mind. I know her face and her smile. I know the way she seemed to float and glide even when she was just walking. She was still the most beautiful woman in the world.

It's been so long since I even looked at a picture of her. My father didn't like to keep many of them around. I think he felt like they anchored him in place. Like if he thought of any one location as where she was, he wouldn't be able to leave it. And he always needed to be able to leave. But I can remember the images of her that used to hang around the house and fill the one album on the shelf in the living room. Even when he was willing to put them on display and look at them constantly, there weren't many pictures of my family, especially him and my mother.

At least, I didn't think there were. It was always understood that taking pictures created a trail. When there was an image of you in a certain place, it links you to that place. It leaves a footprint. People can follow your trail. That was always a threat hanging in the backs of our minds. I never knew why. They never told me, and I didn't ask. Questions also created trails. Once you knew something, there was no way to not know it anymore. That information sat with you and created an invisible tether to all others who knew it. It was safer for me to know nothing and to just go along as I was told.

Yet this box is overflowing with pictures I've never seen. Hundreds of images not kept in any order or contained in books or envelopes. It just looks like somebody took them and tossed them in here to keep them out of sight. The one I'm holding now has my mother laughing in front of a big blue house. She looks young and happy.

"Where is that? What's that house?" Sam asks.

I shake my head. "I don't recognize it. I don't know where that is."

"Do you still have the pictures you took of the papers you got from Iowa?" he asks.

Taking my phone out of my pocket, I pull up the gallery and hand it to him. He scrolls through the images until he gets to the deed to the house. Taking out his own phone, he inputs the address into a mapping website and then turns the screen toward me.

"It's the same house. That's the house in Iowa," I confirm.

I hand Sam the picture of my mother, so I can go through more of the pictures. Several of them are of the exterior of the house, the porch that wraps around it, baskets of flowers hanging from hooks. Others are of a garden in the back and a winding brick path leading to a mailbox. Deeper in the stack, I start finding pictures of the inside. A sudden wave of memory hits me, and I grasp onto Sam's arm.

"What is it?" he asks.

"I know this house," I tell him. "I remember it. It's not much, but I remember being here. This room was the dining room, but it was just the three of us, so we didn't need the formal table and everything. So they emptied it out and turned it into a playroom for me. There was a section of the floor where the stain settled darker, and some of the grain looked like an 'E'."

Flipping through the images faster now, I find a picture of that corner of the floor. "Look. This, right here. My mother said it was a sign. It must have been made just for me." I let out a breath. "I haven't thought about that in so long. I can't believe I remember it."

Sam has reached back into the box for more pictures, and he pauses now, staring at the one in his hands.

"Do you remember this?" he asks, holding one of the pictures out to me.

My breath catches in my throat when I look at it. It's another image of my mother, but this time, she's not alone. Lowered down to her knees on the floor, she has her arm wrapped around my waist, holding me close. I'm very young, barely more than a toddler. Our heads are leaned together as we smile at whoever is taking the picture. I assume my father.

"No," I let out, somewhere between a breath and a whisper. "Sam, look."

My fingertips run across the glossy surface of the picture, brushing over the small section I want him to see. Chains hanging around our necks. Matching pendants resting side by side.

"The necklaces," he says.

I nod. "They were ours. One for my mother, one for me. How did one end up sent to me for my birthday, and one end up under a dead man?"

My phone suddenly ringing startles me. The image gallery Sam consulted disappears, replaced by Eric's name. I answer the call and hold the phone between my ear and shoulder, so I can continue to look through the pictures.

"You have amazing timing," I start. "There's something else I need you to look into for me. I went into the storage unit to look through the stuff left in the house, and I found pictures. Dozens and dozens of pictures, and a lot of them are from the house in Iowa. One of them is of me and my mother wearing..."

"Emma," he cuts me off. "I'm not calling about that."

"What?" I ask. Sam tilts his head to the side to give me a questioning look. "It's Eric," I mouth.

"Something wrong?" he whispers, and I shrug.

"I'm not calling about the stuff you asked me to look into," Eric clarifies.

"Alright. What's going on?"' I ask. "Is everything alright?"

"I'm heading up the team investigating the bombing of the bus station in Richmond," Eric continues.

"I heard about that," I tell him, remembering the brutal news footage. "It's horrible. I didn't realize they called in the Bureau to investigate."

"It's not public knowledge. As you can probably guess, we're not exactly interested in triggering copycats," he sighs.

"If it's not public knowledge, why are you telling me? Is Creagan calling me back from my leave?"

Sam's chin raises slightly, and his shoulders square off subtly. I try not to look directly at him. This is something we'll talk about later. Not right now. The tone in Eric's voice is too strained, too wary for me to dismiss.

"Not exactly. But I do need to show you something," Eric says.

"Alright."

"I've been watching all the surveillance footage from the bombing. Several of the cameras were damaged, and it took some work to get the footage from the others. While I was watching it, I think I saw something. I need you to see it."

"What is it?" I ask.

"I want you to tell me," he says. "I can only send you a small piece through email. This is all that Creagan would approve to be sent. Watch it and tell me if you notice anything."

"Sure," I say.

He ends the call, and a few seconds later, my phone alerts me to a new email. There's no subject line, no message in the body. It's only an attachment with the video clip. I open it and watch through several seconds of uneventful bus station footage. People shuffle around, carrying luggage, rushing for the gates. Hugging their loved ones. My eyes scan over the screen, trying to find what Eric wants me to see. When I do, it hits me so hard I have to lean back against the storage unit wall to hold myself up.

"Emma? What's wrong?" Sam asks.

"It's Greg."

CHAPTER TWENTY

"What do you mean, it's Greg?" Sam asks.

"Greg. My ex-boyfriend," I explain.

"The one who's missing?"

"Well, apparently he's not missing now. Or, at least he wasn't the day the bus station was bombed." I scan back to the beginning of the clip, and Sam steps up beside me to watch. When Greg comes into the shot, I point him out. "Right there."

"Are you sure that's him?" he asks.

"Absolutely," I confirm.

"What is he doing?"

I scramble into action, setting the pictures back into the box and setting the lid on top before sweeping it up onto my hip so I can carry it to the car.

"I don't know, but I need to get home. I need to talk to Eric about this."

"What do you need to talk to him about?" Sam asks.

I stuff the tote into the trunk and slam it closed, looking at him over the top of the car.

"There was a bombing. People died. More are just barely hanging onto life. And a person who hasn't been seen or heard from in two years just walks through the place. What don't you understand about that?" I ask.

I get into the car, and Sam gets behind the wheel, cranking the engine as I watch the video clip again. It's short, less than a minute long. But I watch it over and over. There has to be something else in it. By the time we get back to my house, I've watched the clip so many times I could recreate it by memory. I know the clothes the people around him are wearing. I know the movements they make as he walks through the station. What I don't know is why Greg is there and what he's doing.

Eric answers on the first ring.

"What is he doing there?" I ask.

"You saw him, too," he says.

"Of course I did. What in the hell is Greg doing at that bus station?" I ask.

"We don't know. Piecing together everything that happened that day hasn't been easy."

"Is this the only piece of footage he is in?" I ask.

"No, there's more. He showed up on a couple of the different cameras."

"Can I see more of it?"

"I can't send any more footage over email. That's the only portion Creagan approved. When I pointed Greg out to him, he wanted to make sure. He wanted you to see it and know how you reacted."

"What's that supposed to mean? Does he think I've known where Greg is all this time? That I know why he was at that bus station before it exploded?" I ask defensively.

"He's not accusing you of anything. He's just trying to make sense of all this."

"Then why won't you let me see the rest of the footage?"

"Like I said, we're trying to keep a tight lid on the investigation. Tensions in Richmond are already high because of Jake's case. People are showing up wanting to meet him, leaving flowers on the sidewalk in front of the jail. A couple of times, they've swarmed the jail during meeting hours."

I cringe.

"Serial killer groupies are disgusting," I comment. "I will never understand that compulsion."

"Well, it might make you feel better to know not all the people showing up want to shack up with him. Our contacts there say there've been quite a few wanting to drag him out into the middle of the street for frontier justice," Eric offers.

"At least that's a more logical reaction," I say.

"The thing is, with all that already happening, the bombing only brought more attention to the city. And you know as well as I do that when there's attention…"

"It brings the psychopaths," I complete his sentence.

"And that's the last thing we want to do right now. Creagan is tightly controlling all the footage and any information we're gathering. Some of the footage has images of confirmed-dead victims, and that's catnip to some of these news outlets. Everything has to be kept close to the vest. But he's offered you clearance."

"What?" I ask, surprised by the announcement.

"He wants to make it very clear you are still considered to be on leave and aren't being asked to be a part of the team for the investigation. But he also admits you might have more insight into Greg than the rest of us. You knew him in a different way and might be able to see things in the footage we can't. He's given you clearance to come back to the office and watch the rest of the videos. Purely in a consultant capacity."

"I'll be there," I tell him.

I hang up the phone and see Sam staring at me. My heart sinks as I realize I forgot he even came into the house with me.

"You'll be where?" he asks.

"There's more footage of the bus station that has Greg in it. Creagan is offering me clearance as a consultant to come and see the rest of the videos to find out if I notice anything they aren't," I explain.

"Back to the office?" he asks.

"Yes. He's concerned about the potential for copycats and doesn't want anything getting out. That includes the footage and any of the details of the case. That little piece Eric emailed me was the only bit Creagan is allowing outside the team, so if I'm going to be able to help, I have to go there," I continue.

"Can't they function without you? They are the FBI, aren't they?" he demands.

I'm taken aback by the sudden surge of anger.

"What's wrong with you?" I ask.

"I just don't understand why they need to call you with this. They're the ones who were supposed to be doing the investigation, not you. You're supposed to be on leave."

"Yeah. And I have been for two months. This is the first time they've called me with anything. You're acting like I'm constantly on the phone with them, or they can't do anything without me," I point out.

"It sure seems that way. The minute something serious happens, they're on the phone with you," Sam snips.

"Greg has been missing for almost two years. No one has any idea what happened to him. Then he suddenly showed up on surveillance before a public attack. Why can't you understand why they would want my opinion on this?" I ask.

"I just don't understand what they think you would be able to do. They have an entire team there working on it," he argues.

"And I don't understand why you're so angry," I fire back.

"I only want what's best for you."

"I don't think that's true. I think you only want what's best for you. You can't stand what I do or that I care about it. You've never been able to."

"Can you blame me?" he asks, his voice getting louder.

"You're in law enforcement, Sam. You've had cases that have stayed with you and that you've gone after tirelessly. Even when other people couldn't see what you did."

"But this isn't your case. You said it yourself. They only want you as a consultant," he points out.

"If there's anything I can do to help, I'm going to," I say.

"Why do you have to do this, Emma? Why is it so important for you to go back there and see the footage? Does Greg still matter to you that much? Is this all about him and the way your relationship ended?"

I draw in a breath to keep myself calm, refusing to even give that a response. I get to my feet, intending to go into the kitchen for a drink, but stop when I see the corner of the coffee table.

"The envelope," I say.

"What?" Sam asks.

"The envelope for the papers I got from Iowa. It was sitting on top of the stack of papers when I left this morning. Now it's on the table."

"You must have knocked it off when you sat down."

I shake my head. "No. I didn't."

Scooping up the papers, I sift through them.

"Stop changing the subject," he says.

"My father's certificate of live birth from the midwife is missing. It was right here near the top of the stack, and now it's gone."

"This is exactly what I'm talking about," he laments. "You get yourself so wrapped up in whatever you're investigating; you don't even think about anything else around you. You don't even see what else is happening. All that matters to you is getting that high of the next clue, the next thing to chase."

I glare at him, my jaw set hard enough to make the muscles ache at the hinge.

"Have you been hanging out with Pamela? Wearing your leopard print dress and gossiping with your gal pals? Go ahead. Take it a step further and say you think I've lost my mind," I snap.

"Emma, you're being ridiculous," he says, only making me angrier.

"Just stop," I tell him, walking around the table to go into the kitchen. "You're not making this situation any better."

But Sam persists, following me as he lowers his voice back down.

"I don't think you've lost your mind. But I do think you let yourself get too immersed and need the time to rest. I've seen how these cases have affected you, how much you put yourself into them," he says.

"It's my career. I've put my entire life into it. Of all people, you should know that."

His eyes darken, and he straightens, pulling away from me slightly as his head bobs in a barely perceptible nod.

"I do," he says.

"Then you understand why I have to do this."

Sam shakes his head.

"No, Emma. I don't."

CHAPTER TWENTY-ONE

It's been months since I've worn a suit when I wasn't in court, and I don't think my body has fully acclimated back to it yet. Jeans and t-shirts with my hair slung up in a ponytail are far more my speed. Perhaps the occasional sweater or a dress if the mood strikes me. Suits are reserved for when I have to appear in court for one of my cases, or when I have to meet with my superiors at the office. Especially after I've been gone for a while. I don't want to walk into the office in my favorite shirt I picked up during one of my trips to Florida and have Creagan think I don't have it in me anymore.

The suit also helps to keep my mind from wandering back to Sherwood and to Sam. I'm still aching over our last interaction. We haven't spoken since he walked out of my house after I told him I was coming back here. Not that we had much time to. My bags were packed, and I was on the road less than an hour later. The drive feels shorter than I expected it to, and it's still only the middle of the afternoon when I pull into a welcome center a short distance away from the FBI headquarters. I don't want to go back to my house. Not just yet. Instead, I go into one of the bathrooms and use my time-honored skills honed first by years of theater, then by going undercover, to change into my suit in just seconds. Back in my heels, I stare into the mirror and pull my hair down from its ponytail. Bending at the waist and giving it a puff brings it back to life, and a swipe of mascara wakes up my face.

Just like that, I've shifted back. It's dizzying to think of everything that's happened today. Breakfast with Sam. The confrontation with Payton and Ian. Conversation with Michael Blair. Finding the pictures in the storage unit. Then having my reality shattered and coming back here. It's far too much to crash into the space of just one day, and my mind is still reeling from it. But I can't let it. Not now. I need to get to the office and figure out what we're going to do next.

I try not to be aware of the people around me when I scan my identification and walk into the FBI headquarters. They're looking at me. I know they are. It's only to be expected. After having a crisis and nearly destroying an undercover operation left me confined to spending six months surfing my desk, I fell for and was nearly killed by a serial killer during my very next undercover gig. Considering that was rapidly followed by returning to the hometown no one knew I had, to uncover a kidnapper and ending up on leave, I'm a bit of a point of interest.

It's not that I mind them looking at me. Trying to beat the hell out of a drug dealer and suspected child sex ring monster while in a moving vehicle wasn't the first time I've drifted over to the side of going rogue. Frankly, it probably won't be my last. I'm used to the looks and the whispers. It's just that now is not the time to play catchup. I need to get to Eric and bantering with colleagues I barely know who will pry into my life under the guise of checking in on me is a speed bump I'm not interested in dealing with.

Walking through the building is a homecoming of sorts. These last two months in Sherwood have been the longest I've been away from the headquarters since I became an agent. It feels good to be back, even if it's in circumstances I could never have imagined.

Eric gets up from his chair and gathers me in a hug as soon as he sees me.

"I can't believe you got here so fast," he says.

"Of course I did." I nod at the two other agents sitting at the table in front of a bank of television screens. "Hey, guys."

"Good to see you back," Smith says.

"It hasn't been the same around here without you pushing Creagan toward early retirement," Maloney laughs.

"Don't get too attached to her," Eric warns. "Remember, she's only here as a consultant. According to Creagan, she is still on leave and will be sent right back to bucolic Sherwood when she's done here."

"Just be sure to ship me overnight express," I tell him sarcastically. "You don't want me in that crate for too long."

"Oh, don't worry. The weather's getting cooler. You'll be just fine," he responds.

I make a face at him, but the humor doesn't last long. The reality of why I'm here settles back in.

"Tell me about the rest of the footage," I say.

"We're sifting through all of the different cameras to see how many instances of Greg showing up we can isolate. The clip I sent you is from when he first walked into the bus station. Here's the rest of it."

Eric pulls up the same footage as he sent me, and I watch it through again. Only this time, it continues on past the thirty-five seconds he sent.

"Whatever he's doing, he seems determined to do it," I note.

"We noticed that, too. He's not just wandering around. He doesn't look confused or anxious. He goes into the station, walks right through, and heads toward the back. This is about forty minutes before the bomb went off. Now, look at this. It's from another camera. Watch right in this upper corner."

The footage starts again, and I notice it's a camera pointed at the bank of lockers toward the back of the station. I focus on the area Eric pointed out to me, and several seconds into the feed notice Greg appear from around a corner at the top of the screen. Now he's holding a large dark green duffel bag.

"That bag," I frown, pointing to it. "He didn't have that when he came in."

"I know. So, the question is, what's in it and where did he get it?" Eric asks.

"What's around that corner? Where did he come from?" I ask.

"Nothing. There's some bathrooms, a storage area only the maintenance people have access to, and an emergency exit."

I watch Greg move through the crowd and stop in front of the lockers. He crouches down and is temporarily out of sight as people stand in front of him. A few seconds later, he stands back up and folds the now-empty duffel bag.

"He put something in the locker," I say. "But we don't know which one."

"Right. Now watch what he does."

Without looking around him or even seeming to notice there are other people near him, he walks back around the corner and down the hallway.

"When was this?"

"About half an hour before the explosion," Eric says.

"So, wherever he was, he was back there for around ten minutes."

"Right. And he does it again. This time, it's fifteen."

"What could he be doing back there?" I ask.

Eric shrugs. "Now, this is from another camera. It's not much, so you have to watch closely."

Greg's form appears again, standing at the back of the station and staring out over the people there. He seems to be waiting for something. A few moments later, he walks out of the frame.

"Where did he go?" I ask.

"That's the thing. We're not sure. The next footage we have is about fifteen minutes later."

"At the time of the explosion," I say quietly.

Eric pulls up the footage. It seems to be the same camera from the first clip of him or one close to it. He's walking back toward the front of the station, staying close to the side nearest the buses. He's almost at the door when the camera catches the sound of the explosion, the flash of red light, then shuts off.

"That's it?" I ask, pointing at the screen and looking at Eric in shock. "There's nothing else?"

"No. A couple of the cameras survived the blast enough to keep recording, but it's just chaos. He doesn't show up in any of them."

"How about the cameras in front of the bus station or in the parking lot?" I ask. "Did any of them get him coming out?"

"The only cameras focused on the front door are the ones inside. The cameras outside cover some of the parking lot. Not the whole thing but a good portion of it. He doesn't show up in any of them," Eric tells me.

I sag in my seat, trying to let it all roll through my mind and sink in. After a few seconds, I look back over at Eric.

"Did Greg do this?" I ask.

"We don't know, Emma."

"Do you think he did?"

"We don't know what happened. That's what we're trying to figure out," he tells me.

It's not really an answer to my question, but it's all I'm going to get. I sit back up.

"Show it all to me again."

CHAPTER TWENTY-TWO

FOUR YEARS AGO

She couldn't eat the apples anymore. Not since she saw the man tied to the tree. She wasn't supposed to see him. Looking out the window meant she was distracted, that she wasn't putting all of herself into what she was meant to be doing. That night it was stitching her blanket. Each woman created one, a unique piece designed by her and stitched by hand. She'd been working on hers for almost a month, and it was nearly done. Her stitches were tiny and even, the pattern flowing and smooth to remind her of air. But the long hours spent hunched over in the glow of the oil lamps, the only light they were allowed, made her back ache and her mind fog.

She didn't want it to. She fought for her mind to stay clear and maintain the absolute focus she was meant to. Thinking of anything else was weakness, a flaw that could make her deemed unworthy. That couldn't happen. Not now. But that night she couldn't help but take a moment to herself. She pulled her thoughts and concentration away from the blanket forming under her hands and glanced through the window to her side. She was surprised at how late it was. The hours went by without anyone coming to stop her, to offer food, to speak a single word to her. The only passage of time was the darkness of the room deepening and her eyes becoming more dependent on the light of the lamp. She was accustomed to that now. Light barely touched her anymore.

She was to become the light. She didn't need it given to her. Even the lamp was a luxury granted with the reminder it could be taken away just as easily. She was to create the light within herself. It was her role, her place. She was called to be the light for others, for Lucas.

Outside, the only light came from the moon. Even the stars were hidden behind clouds stretched like dyed wool across the sky. She almost didn't notice him. She almost turned back to the breath of air across the blue fabric draped on her lap. If he hadn't lifted his head, she would have. It was only a slight movement. His chin rose up from where it rested on his chest just enough that his eyes would be able to see above the ground. An instant later, it fell back. His body sagged against the ropes lashed around him. In seconds it was obvious the tension of the rough cords was the only thing holding him up.

She ached to see breath. She held her own like it might somehow give it to him. He wore nothing above his waist; his skin marred with deep lines and discoloration. She wanted to look away, but she couldn't. Something inside her told her the moment she did; he wouldn't exist anymore. That's how it was within The Tower.

Finally, two other men came to the tree and cut the ropes away. He toppled forward, and they let him fall to the ground. She imagined his blood soaking into the ground and being drawn up into a tree's roots. They picked him up and dragged him away. She didn't know his name. She never had to.

The next morning, she could only wonder how many men's blood were within the apples ground down for their cider.

Two weeks later, she put the final stitch in her blanket. It was beautiful, and she looked forward to draping it across her bed. It would give her something new to look at, a reminder that there was loveliness and hope to come. But when she brought it to Ruth, to show she had finished what she'd been told to do, she wasn't allowed to bring the blanket to her room.

She was brought into the core of The Tower, led to a room with a steaming bath sunken into the floor. Her hair hung long and loose now, no longer braided like the women first brought into the Society. Two other women, their hair twisted in tight buns at the backs of their heads and their wrists encircled with bright scars, brushed through the long strands, then undressed her. Without a word of explanation, they bathed her and rubbed oil into her skin. The brand on her waist no longer hurt when the water touched it, but she still hadn't gotten used to the way it felt, so rough and protruding against the rest of her skin.

As they draped her in pale blue gossamer and strung her neck with gold, she knew what was happening. They were preparing her for sacrifice.

The blanket she crafted, designed by her spirit, stitched with her hopes and devotion, imbued with her blood, wasn't for her. It would never be on her bed. It was made as a gift to present to Lucas. Ruth brought her into a massive bedroom lined with heavy wood wardrobes, their doors open. Inside were rows of blankets hanging from hooks.

"Congratulations, Sister Abigail," Ruth said, carrying the blanket over to the bed at the side of the room and resting it on the crisp white sheets. "Your first phase of the Circle of Light purified you and warmed your spirit. You have learned to be a light for yourself and a light unto others. Tonight, you fulfill your ultimate purpose and become a light for Lucas."

She shook her head.

"I don't understand," she said.

Ruth looked at her through eyes that had seen so many standing in just the place she was. *Yes, you do,* those eyes said. But her lips curved into a soft smile. That smile crept through her veins and wrapped in a coil around her heart. It was always that smile. That smile came before the lesson. It came before needles pressed into her fingertips over and over so she would be prepared to stitch. It came before missed meals and hours washing what was already clean. It came before people left The Tower, and she came to stroke her hair and remind her to guard herself from The Existence or fear losing her place in the New Time.

"Everyone must work together to bring about the New Time, Sister Abigail. Everyone within our Society has within them a special task, a role that is essential to creating the glorious future that awaits us. Lucas's role is the most important, the most valuable. You were chosen and have been nurtured until now to be in the Circle of Light, his gathering of treasures. You will be his light, and he will cherish you. This will give him strength and connect his spirit to The Essence. Through this, he will lead us all into what has been promised to us."

She remembered Sister Clarissa with her long copper-colored hair and blood on her lips. She was there for a brief time after she was brought into the Circle. All the women in the Circle lived together in a separate section of The Tower, away from where they lived before they were brought through the ceremony. For a few weeks, they spent time together, but then she was gone. She never asked.

Never ask. Never question. Now she wondered which of the blankets was Sister Clarissa's, and where she would be brought when the night was through, and hers was hung on the empty hook in the wardrobe across the room.

CHAPTER TWENTY-THREE

NOW

I press the mask closer to my face to make it easier to breathe as we pick our way through the wreckage of the bus station. Even after the time that's passed, there's still so much dust and debris in the air in some areas; it makes breathing feel like choking. Occasionally the crews working on cleaning up the destruction move something that sends another gust of crumbled concrete and dirt into our eyes.

It's strange to be working in a crime scene that's also being demolished around us as we speak. It's like we are working against time. Ideally, we would have everything kept exactly as it was the day of the explosion, but that just isn't an option. The bus station is set in a busy area of this city, and having a crumbling building is a threat against public safety. We have to make do with the extensive photographs, surveillance camera footage, and picking our way through the scene itself, hoping to uncover its secrets as it's dismantled around us.

Yesterday there were piles of stuffed animals and flowers stacked just beyond the orange plastic fencing set up to block access to the site. Tributes for the lives lost in the wreckage just feet away. Some of the survivors who managed to get through the incident without serious injury stood there staring at what was left of the building.

There's always a haunted look to the face of someone who has walked through a brush with death. They're called survivors and celebrated for making it through the horrible incident. But that's not really true. No one ever really survives something like this. Human beings may walk out of the building, and others may be released from the hospital in the days and weeks following. They may still be breathing, and they may continue on for years. But those are not the same people who walked into the building that morning. No one can watch an explosion tear apart a couple kissing after being reunited after weeks apart or be splattered by the blood of someone's arm being blown off right beside them, and really survive.

They are different people when it's all over. Some can go back to the lives they lived. They can seem the same in nearly every way, but there's always going to be a part of them lying dead in the ashes.

"That's where the lockers were?" I ask, pointing to a pile of mangled metal and cracked concrete several feet ahead.

"Yes," Eric nods. "Only a few of them were still standing. Mostly the ones to the very far back."

"Do you think that's where the bomb was planted? Someone put it in a locker and waited for it to go off?" I ask.

I don't say Greg's name. I'm not going to make that assumption.

"We don't know that for sure. The experts are still analyzing all the information we have, to try to pinpoint exactly where the explosive detonated. Right now, we can't even say for sure it was only one site," Eric says.

"You think it could have been more than one set of explosives?" I ask.

"It's possible. It would be hard to bring in something of this type of magnitude without someone noticing something. But if it was several smaller devices, it would be easier for someone to bring them in and set them up," he says.

"Like in a green duffel bag?" I mutter lowly.

"Emma, that's not what I'm saying."

"I just want your reassurance the team hasn't zeroed in on him and are just going to assume he did it," I say.

"I promise that's not what's happening. The truth is, nobody knows why Greg was here that day or what he was doing. We don't know if he has anything to do with this at all. We have to look into all the possibilities."

"Then why don't we go see if we can find out what's behind door number three," I say, pointing toward the corner ahead of us.

Along with the front of the building, this section of the bus station seems to be the least fazed by the explosion. Some of the blocks making up the wall are broken, and the walls and floor are smeared with smoke and soot. But the majority of the structure is still standing. We pick through the broken bits of the building until we get to the corner we saw Greg walk around in the security footage. According to the map of the building, the short hallway after the corner should only have a restroom, a storage closet, and an emergency exit. But Greg came down this hallway twice during his time at the bus station before the explosion went off. Once for ten minutes and once for nearly fifteen. The first time, he came back with the duffel bag. There has to be something back here we're missing.

"We've talked to a few witnesses," Eric says, "and nobody can remember being in the men's bathroom during that time frame before the explosion. But we do have an eyewitness who was standing outside the ladies room. She said that she had the door standing partially open and was halfway in the hallway and halfway in the bathroom."

"Somebody should tell her that's not how it's done," I say.

Eric rolls his eyes at me. "She was waiting for a small child who wanted to exert some independence. She doesn't remember seeing anyone go in or out of the bathroom the entire time she was standing there. We can't corroborate that conclusively, of course. We were able to find her on the surveillance camera going down that hallway with a little girl about twenty-five minutes before the explosion but have no footage of her coming back. It's entirely possible she's concealed behind other people, and we just missed her, but we can't use her statement in absolutes."

"But it's something," I say.

"It is. But it also brings up another question. If she didn't see Greg go into the bathroom, where did he go? She didn't mention seeing a man in the hallway at all. I think if she was trying to cooperate with the authorities investigating to what equates to a terror attack where she was with her child, she would give every detail she possibly could," he says.

"Possibly. But you also have to keep in mind the trauma she went through. You ask her very specific questions, and she might have given you a very specific answer. You wanted to know if she saw him and go into or out of the bathroom while she was standing in the hallway. Maybe she only thought about that specific element of her standing there. You instilled in her mind that it's the bathroom itself that's important, not the area of the bus station. I suggest you talk to her again and broaden out what she saw."

"You're right," he nods. "I will." His phone rings in the front pocket of his suit, and he pulls it out, turning his back as he answers it. His head straightens, and he peaks over his shoulder at me. "Yeah, she's here."

When he turns and walks toward me with his hand extended.

"It's Creagan. He says if he wasn't at work and didn't need to maintain his professionalism, he would tell you to turn your fucking phone on so he could fucking get in touch with you," he says.

"I'm so glad he was able to restrain himself," I roll my eyes, taking the phone from Eric's hand.

"I only have my personal phone with me, and I didn't want to have that possibly ring while I was in the field," I start, without even bothering to greet him. Creagan rarely has time for frivolous things like manners.

"You should have your personal phone on right now because you are on your personal time," he says in a gravelly voice.

"What do you mean?" I ask.

"When Eric showed me that footage and said he wanted to run it past you because of Greg, I thought it was a good idea. But only if you fully understood it was in a consultant capacity only. You are not on this case. You should not be investigating anything. So imagine my surprise when I went to the office to catch up with you and Smith told me you and Eric hopped a plane on the Bureau's dime so you could do some sightseeing in Richmond," Creagan says, his tone getting angrier.

"We aren't sightseeing," I protest.

"Are you on the team investigating this case?"

"No."

"Did I give either of you permission to go back to the site?"

"No."

"Sightseeing."

Eric takes the phone and puts it on speaker so we can both talk.

"With all due respect, sir, I am the lead on this case. It was my call to come to the site."

"You may be the lead on the case, but you still go through me. I made it very clear to you that Griffin was not on this investigation."

"Why can't I be?" I ask. "Why should I have to stay out of the investigation?"

"You're too close. We don't know where Greg is, what might have happened to him, or what he might be involved in. The things we might uncover during this investigation could be upsetting," he says.

"I can handle it. I think I've proven my ability to manage difficult cases," I argue.

"Not like this, Griffin. This is different," he says.

"Why?" I ask.

"Because in those cases, the people you're investigating haven't been a part of your life for years," Creagan tells me flatly.

The comment makes me take a moment.

"Are you questioning my integrity?" I ask. "You think if I found out Greg was involved in something, I wouldn't be able to hold him accountable for it? Or is it that you think because he broke up with me, I would try to pin something on him as some kind of revenge?"

"I'm not saying any of that. I'm just saying it's better if you leave this to people without the baggage. You're not to be a part of this investigation. That's an order."

CHAPTER TWENTY-FOUR

"Now I owe the FBI $300."

Bellamy drops down on the couch next to me and settles a massive bowl of popcorn into my lap. She takes a swig of the cream soda she's holding, and I cringe. She's had a particular passion for the sickly-sweet drink as long as I've known her. I've never craved a plate of green vegetables quite as much as the time she made an ice cream float with cream soda and topped it with whipped cream. I can binge with the best of them, but that's taking things a few two steps too far into Candyland territory for me.

"Do you actually think Creagan is going to call you in on that?" she asks.

"Oh, I think Creagan would be willing to make me put on a blue polyester A-line dress and play it off as being a flight attendant. At least it would keep me out of his hair for a while," I tell her. "I just can't believe he's being so incredibly unreasonable about this investigation. Of everybody in the Bureau, I knew Greg the best. So, shouldn't I be the one who's trying to figure out where he went and what he's been doing?"

"I don't know," she says.

I look at her in disbelief.

"You agree with him?" I ask.

"I just said I don't know. It's a really strange situation. This isn't like your father. His work with the CIA meant most of his life was one big secret. You guys had to move and run and stay out of sight all the time. Him being gone for this many years is unprecedented, but it's not as completely out of character as it is with Greg. Greg is predictable and steady to a fault. He is also likely one of the most boring agents in the history of the Bureau."

I shoot her a look. Greg and I are ancient history, sure, but still.

"What? It's true. You know I'm right. He isn't like all these guys who fight and clamor to get on the big investigations. He didn't want to go out in the field or do undercover work. You know he doesn't care about serial killers or terrorist attacks. He has always been perfectly happy to stay at headquarters and look into cybercrime and fraud. You are the most interesting thing he's ever associated with, and even his relationship with you was straightforward and predictable and safe."

I shoot her the same look again.

"No offense," she tries, only half meaning it. She clearly is loving putting me on the defensive here. She takes another swig of her cream soda and continues.

"But just all of a sudden, he decides he's going to break up with you for no reason, then disappear out into nowhere? That's just not the type of person he is. Something else has to be going on, and because of your history, you just might not be the right person to be digging into it."

"Is," I say.

She looks at me strangely.

"What?"

"You said 'is'. When you were talking about my father, you talked about him in the past tense. But with Greg, you are still talking about in the present," I clarify.

Color flushes against her cheeks, and she invests herself in another deep swig of her cream soda.

"I'm sorry," she says. "I should be more careful with what I say. I didn't mean..."

I shake my head. "It's alright. I understand. He's been gone for ten years. Most people would want to talk about him in the past tense, too. It just makes more sense that way. I just hate to think about it," I tell her. "Besides, I'm starting to wonder if all that running really was about the CIA."

"What do you mean?"

"I know some of it had to do with his work. I never got any details or anything, but I heard my parents talking about it, and when he was gone, sometimes men he worked with would come over to check on us. But there were other times when he would leave, or we would have to hurry off without any warning or preparation. They seemed so much more on edge during those times. It was like they were afraid of something. I can't help but wonder if there was something else going on," I say.

"What do you think could be going on?" she asks.

"I don't know. But lately, I've..." my voice trails off, and I shake my head.

"What? Lately you've been what?" she asks.

"The people in Sherwood think I have gone crazy," I sigh. "And think I went back there, and I'm taking time off because I broke and haven't been glued back together yet."

"Well, they just don't know you like I do," Bellamy says.

"Thanks," I try to smile.

"You cracked a long time ago. We've all gotten used to it." She grins, and I swat at her with one of the throw pillows on the couch.

"I'm serious," I say, my face falling back down to neutral. "What if they're right and I just don't realize it? I've started seeing him."

"Seeing who? Sam?" she asks.

"My father," I say.

Her face doesn't change expressions for a few seconds.

"Your father?" she asks.

"I told you. It sounds ridiculous. But there's been a couple of times when I looked up, and I saw a man, and for a brief second, I could have sworn it was him."

"Have you ever said anything to him?"

"No. And he's never said anything to me, either. As soon as I look at him, he just walks away. It's like I miss him so much, and I want to know what happened so badly I've just started superimposing him over other people's faces. I'm just making it up whenever I feel like it," I say.

"That's normal," she says, pressing her lips into a tight line and offering her hand to mine. She squeezes my fingers softly. "You never got a chance to grieve for your father. Whether he's..."

"Past or present tense?" I offer.

She nods. "Either way, it doesn't matter. He's not here and hasn't been for a long time. Any type of separation like that needs grief. You have to grieve the relationship you had and the man you knew. You have to grieve for all the time that you've missed together. You've never given yourself the opportunity to do that. It's possible that now, especially being back in Sherwood, your mind is kind of trying to force you to do it."

A few days later, I'm back on a plane to Richmond. Only this time, it's legitimately paid for by the Bureau. I'm not going to check in on the investigation into Greg or even look at the bus station. This time I'm there for a hearing in Jake's case. It's not something I've been looking forward to, but at the same time, I'm glad it's finally here. The more hearings I get through, the closer I am to having the entire mess over with so I can just put it behind me.

Riding up to the courthouse, I see exactly what Eric was talking about when he described the people flooding to the city because of Jake. Police have set up barricades and are standing on either end of sidewalks and in the streets, doing the best they can to control the crowds. Some of the people gather there to shout threats and hold up signs describing various methods of public execution they would like to reinstate just for Jake's benefit. The more subdued protesters simply stand there, holding up poster-sized pictures of the victims. Looking at some of them still takes my breath away. I stood right beside their bodies. I touched some of them. But I wouldn't have been able to recognize some of them just by picture alone. Jake did his best to preserve them, but too many were destroyed by decay or taken apart for parts.

The other half of the crowd is the complete opposite. Women scream like fans gathered outside the back door at a concert, waiting to be that city's flavor of the night. Some stand to gather in a circle holding hands, singing something that could be a hymn. I'd really like to think they're singing for the victims, but I've done this enough to know they're not. They see Jake as something far more powerful than he is. That is what's scary about Jake. Not what he did, but what he has the capacity to do. Compelling and charismatic, smart and creative. He has the ability to draw people in and give them exactly what they need without them ever realizing what's happening to them.

Creagan managed to convince me to have a fifteen-minute sit down with my therapist yesterday. I'm not about to start peeling back my layers again. Not right now, anyway. But a fifteen-minute session to prepare me for today was a compromise I could live with. She asked me if I was ready for today. She thinks the same way most people do. They expect me to be terrified to walk into the courtroom with him. I should be scared or uncomfortable. Some wonder why I don't cry.

I won't pretend it doesn't affect me to see him. There's no way it couldn't. But for every bit of fear and hesitation that comes over me, I push back. I fought for myself, and I pushed back for every one of the people who didn't get the chance to walk away from him. He is the type of man who could convince people to trust him again, and while I will always lay a heavy portion of the blame for what happened to the devastation of his past, I will stand in the way to stop anyone from being fooled by him again.

The hearing goes as well as could be expected. I sit in the witness chair and talk about my role as an undercover agent. I explain what I witnessed and how I uncovered the truth about the secrets in Feathered Nest. It's not the last time I'm going to have to tell the story. I know that. But each time I do is cathartic. I remind the world of what really happened. I get to say their names.

At the end of the hearing, I walk out of the courtroom and past the reporters trying to catch a sound bite. I get down the steps when ahead of me, I notice a familiar form. It surprises me enough to me to question if I'm actually seeing it accurately. Then he turns around, and I know it's him.

"Sam?" I call. He pauses and gives me the time to jog up to him. "What are you doing here?"

"I told you I'd be here. I promised I would be at all the hearings," he shrugs. "So, I'm here."

"Thank you. It means so much to me to know you were here. I wish I'd known you were here before I went in there," I say. "Look, I really wanted to say I'm sorry about the way things were between us before I left. I'd love to get something to eat and talk."

"I can't. I only came into town for this because I said I would be here. But I've got to get back."

Sam cups his hand behind the back of my neck and pulls me in to kiss my forehead. Without another word, he turns and walks away.

I end up in my hotel room an hour later sitting on the bed and picking at a room service tuna melt that isn't nearly as satisfying as the pizza I wanted to order. The news comes on, and a picture of Everly Zara appears on the screen. I turn up the volume.

"Though he declined to share any specific details, Sheriff Samuel Johnson of Sherwood now confirms the death of Everly Zara was not a suicide as originally assumed. Her death by hanging at her home is now being investigated as a murder."

CHAPTER TWENTY-FIVE

THREE AND A HALF YEARS AGO

The gardens were so beautiful. Candles glowed like fireflies inside the lanterns strung on the branches of the trees, filling the air with sweet scented smoke. Music played from somewhere, but she couldn't see it. It felt like the notes were coming out of the leaves and flowers themselves. It was almost like heaven.

But it wasn't. It couldn't be. Not here. Not at The Tower.

The dress she wore was barely thick enough to keep away the chill despite the warm evening. When the breeze picked up, it sank through the fabric and pressed into her skin, revealing every detail of her body to the men who walked around her. They wore masks, but it wasn't hard to see their eyes. They traced the outlines of the women through the thin fabric, fixating on shadows and delving into hidden dips.

"Welcome," Lucas called out over the sound of the music and the voices of those milling through the garden.

She looked up and saw him standing on a platform built like an altar. Exalting himself. Praying to himself. Preying on them.

Lucas smiled brightly; his hands held out to his sides away from the white robe he wore.

"Honored friends, thank you for joining me tonight. Welcome to our home and to my Circle of Light. I've invited you here to celebrate what is coming. Can you feel the change? All around you, it's happening. I've been waiting, devoting myself, fasting. Offering myself up as a vessel. As the world has moved around me, I've stayed vigilant, knowing it would come. Now it is drawing near. The New Time is at hand. Tonight, we welcome it. We come together to taste of the fruits of what our paradise will bring. Our Society has given of ourselves for what will be for all those chosen. We're ready to take what is ours and welcome you to feast with us. Enjoy yourselves! My treasures will light your way."

A hand wrapped around her wrist. She turned to see a mask inches from her face. The eyes peering back at her were wide and so pale blue they looked nearly white. The color made her stomach turn, but her face stayed calm. There was nothing she could do now. He selected her. This man with no face, with no name. Lucas presented her and the other women as his gift to them, and there was nothing she could do to refuse.

As the man brought a glass to her lips and tipped burning wine down her throat, she saw the men from The Tower walk into the garden. They walked in a line, their backs straight, their hands clasped in front of them. She nearly gagged on the sickly liquid when she saw Jeremiah. She wanted to scream out to him, to run to him, but her feet didn't move. It would mean nothing. This was the first time she had seen his face in three months.

Maybe he didn't know. He didn't understand. And yet, she knew he did. He stood there among the other men, bracelets crossed over bare wrists, emotionless faces watching the masked men make their selections. His eyes brushed over her like she wasn't even there. She faded with that gaze.

The garden was less beautiful when she walked back into it. The masked man had already returned and walked the waving paths with another glass of wine and a plate of the same decadent treats Eloise made the day she first came to The Tower.

The bath Ruth insisted she take kept her out of the garden for a few extra minutes. She was thankful for them, but they didn't last long. Another pair of eyes behind a featureless white mask caught hold of her. It might as well have been a vice. They held her in place as he walked toward her and stroked his fingertips along a collarbone still damp from the rose-scented water.

By the fifth time she walked into the sunken bath, the stone bottom of the tub felt slick and slimy with the rose petals that sank down. Women with tight buns and downcast eyes sprinkled fresh petals onto the surface after every few girls, but nothing could sweeten the water.

Thirty-six hours later, she lay on the side of the bath, her face pressed against the stone. The petals were gone, and new water rushed into the empty tub. One of the women reached for the buttons on her dress, and she groaned. The woman reached again, and she used every bit of energy she could to turn herself away. The attendants disappeared, and in the few seconds of quiet and emptiness in the room, the water called to her. Before she could slide over the side, heavy footsteps stormed into the room.

"Sister Abigail, Chloe and Vivian tell me you refuse to bathe," said Ruth, her voice shocked as if she couldn't imagine the thought.

"I'm so tired," she told her.

"Come along. The bath will revive you. Lucas is waiting."

She sobbed at the sound of his name, curling her body in closer.

"No," she said.

"Excuse me?"

"No," she said again, her voice little more than a whimper.

"Sister Abigail, Lucas selected your blanket tonight. I spread it on his bed. You've already kept him waiting. He's willing to be lenient with you tonight because you were so welcoming to his guests at his event, but I cannot promise you that he will maintain his gentle nature for long. He doesn't respond well to disrespect."

"I can't," she said. "Please. I can't."

"Of course, you can. Get into the bath. Chloe and Vivian will help you. I will speak to Lucas and tell him you won't be much longer."

"No. I can't. This wasn't supposed to be this way."

Ruth took slow steps toward her, stopping only inches from her head, staring down into her face. Completely silent. Her foot turned just enough to catch her hair and pin it down to the stone, pulling it so sharp pain radiated through her scalp. She gasped and tried to move away, but Ruth had her firmly.

"We all have to give of ourselves for the future, Sister Abigail. We must purge ourselves of the weakness and corruption of The Existence, so we are purified and worthy for the New Time. Only those who are worthy will live in the paradise Lucas is ushering in for us. It is not for the selfish and the wicked. It is not for the unfaithful. You were chosen. He saw value in you. He deemed you ready to be molded into a treasure for him. It is your duty to offer yourself so Lucas can channel The Essence and create light for the new creation."

"And to those other men?" she asked.

Ruth's slap drew blood from her chapped, worn lips.

"Let that be a reminder to you of the pain and torment you bring to all those driven and aching for the future. When you refuse to obey and put yourself above them, above Lucas, you condemn us all to longer in The Existence. It is not up to you to understand how Lucas brings us forward or the ways that he connects his being to The Essence for the good of all of us. I won't have him waiting on you any longer. Take off your dress so you can ready yourself for him."

"No," she begged.

"Then you will keep it on," Ruth scowled.

Her foot lifted from her hair, and a hard kick sent her toppling into the water. She fought to come to the surface, but her exhausted body and clouded mind couldn't push back against Ruth holding her down. Her head hit the side of the tub, and more blood seeped into the water. Her body went limp, but just before the water drained into her lungs, hands wrenched her out.

She didn't know how the men got into the room so quickly or what Ruth told them. It all went by in a blur. But she felt them carrying her down steep, winding steps. She clawed for the banister with all the strength she could find, but the wood peeled away her thin, weakened skin. Finally, there was nothing more she could do. They brought her beneath The Tower where there was nothing but a choking, suffocating smell and the sound of something scraping the stone floor.

She crashed to the ground so hard she was sure her hip was broken. The men turned and stomped away, slamming the door behind them with a deep, resolute thud.

And then she was alone. Everything around her was pitch black. Her hand reached out and touched something wet. She couldn't breathe the air around her. The smell choked every bit of oxygen from her. She tried to crawl forward, but the clang of metal stopped her. She realized she was in a cell.

A few seconds later, a flame appeared in the blackness. It glowed on Jeremiah's face, his expression a scowl as he lit a lamp and hung it on a hook outside the door.

"One month to purge. Then you must purify yourself again," he muttered.

She tried to call after him, but he said nothing more. His eyes lingered on her for only a moment, but he walked away.

She could make no sound. Pulling herself back, she turned, and her scream found her. It ricocheted from the stone and rained back down from the ceiling, falling on long red hair matted with blood and skin falling away from bones. Her whisper would never be heard.

"Sister Clarissa."

CHAPTER TWENTY-SIX

NOW

"Why didn't you tell me?" I ask, holding my phone with my shoulder as I take off my shoes.

"Honestly, I didn't think you would care," Sam says. "You have enough going on."

"You didn't think I would care that the suicide I said was suspicious from the very beginning turned out to be murder?" I sputter incredulously.

"Like I said, I figured you already have enough going on. It wouldn't matter to you what was going on around here," he says.

"Of course I care what's going on around there. Just because I needed to come back here for a little while and handle some things doesn't mean I don't care about what's going on there. Especially this."

"Well, that's good to hear."

I let out an exasperated sound.

"You know that's not what I meant," I say. "It doesn't matter. I got an early flight, and I'm on my way back. I'm going through security in Richmond right now. I should be landing in DC in less than two hours, and I'll start the drive back to Sherwood."

"Why would you do that?" he asks.

"What do you mean, why would I do that? I want to know what's going on. I want to help with Everly's case," I tell him.

"What about the bombing?"

"That's not my investigation. They brought me in as a consultant to watch the videos and give them my opinion. That's what I did. Now I'm done, so I'm headed back. It'll be late when I get there, but I'll see you first thing in the morning."

Ending the call, I toss my phone into the container with my carry-on bag, put my shoes on the conveyor belt, and head through the security terminal. I'm cutting it close. It wasn't easy switching the flight I had scheduled for tomorrow morning to the next one flying, but as soon as I heard the news report about Everly, I knew I couldn't stay away for another night. But that meant throwing everything into my luggage, hoping I didn't leave something vital behind and making a run for the airport that would make the McAlister's proud.

I make it to the gate by the skin of my teeth. The attendant checks my boarding pass and issues me a look of decided frustration as she points down the loading ramp. It feels like the plane starts taxing down the runway as soon as I squeeze myself down into the middle seat that was the only thing left when I booked the flight. Both passengers on either side of me are clearly displeased to have me joining them. Both just large enough to be uncomfortable when I put down my armrests, they exchange a glance that tells me they pre-booked and selected their seats with the intention of the seat being empty throughout the flight.

If I wasn't so anxious to get back to Sherwood, I might feel guilty. At the moment, I'm far from it. Being able to snag this seat at the last minute means I don't have to wait another eighteen hours to find out about the investigation into Everly's death. I keep my laptop poised and ready on my lap until we've reached elevation, then pop it open and connect to the Wi-Fi.

A flight between Richmond and DC is just long enough for me to read through the news articles hastily written since Sam's announcement of the murder investigation. There's very little in the way of new information. He's playing it smart and keeping what they know confidential. That's almost always the best strategy when it comes to investigating a murder. Too often, even a seemingly minor detail can tip off the killer and give them the opportunity to cover their tracks.

It's almost two in the morning by the time I finally pull into the driveway. I hesitate in the car for a few seconds, trying to remind myself which lights I purposely left on. They weren't meant to make it look like I was at home. Anybody who lives on the street knows I've been gone for over a week, and my car not being in the driveway is a fairly blatant indication I'm not there. Instead, I left the lights on to make sure they were still on when I got back.

For most people, turning a light off when they leave a room is an impulse. It's so ingrained into what they do on a daily basis unless there's another person actively using the room, as they leave, they reach up and flip the switch. If the lights I chose aren't on, it means someone was in my house while I was gone.

From the driveway, I can see the light burning in my kitchen and the other in my bedroom. The one in the attic would be more difficult to see because the only window not blocked by shutters is a small round cutout near the peak of the roof. But no matter how long I stare at it, I can't detect any glow from the overhead bulb I left on.

Gripping my phone tightly in my hand, I step out of my car and leave the door open. That leaves the cabin light on. A safety tactic that means if I don't come back within the next few minutes to close the door, it will call the attention of one of my neighbors, who can then alert Sam. It's unlikely at this hour that any of my neighbors are awake and peering out windows, but if there is a safety measure I can put into place, I'm going to do it.

The house is quiet when I step inside the front door. Walking through the house, I carefully check each room, every closet, and under my bed. When I'm confident it's empty, I go to the attic door and open it. There's only darkness overhead. I stay still and quiet, listening for any sounds of someone shifting or moving against the wooden floor. When there's nothing, I feel for the light switch beside the door. When my fingers touch it, I realize it's still in the up position. Flicking it up and down several times does nothing, and I let out a long breath, shaking my head.

"I seriously need to get up on my home maintenance priorities," I mutter to myself as I head to the laundry room to get another of the new light bulbs. Getting back to the bottom of the steps, I decide it's too late to climb up into the dark, dusty attic and try to change the lightbulb right now. Or maybe it's too early. Either way, I'll leave it for the next day. I set the light bulb on the steps and close the door behind me. I go outside to shut and lock my car and then go back in the house, securing the front door behind me.

M y alarm wakes me up four hours later. It's just enough time for me to take a fast shower and get dressed so I can make it over to the police station for Sam's arrival. I get there just as he's crossing the parking lot. He looks up from a notebook he's holding but doesn't look particularly thrilled to see me.

"Good morning," I say.

"Morning," he grumbles.

That's the extent of our interaction until we get back into the conference room. Pictures and folders of documents take up a good portion of the oblong table in the center of the room. It's the evidence for the murder investigation, and I'm immediately drawn to it.

"What did you find out?" I ask, heading for the table.

"Emma," he frowns. I don't like the tone of his voice, and I stop to look at him. "I haven't authorized you to be a part of this investigation yet."

"Sam, I can help," I insist.

"I know that. But I can't entrust you with something this delicate and important if I can't be sure you are going to see it through," he says.

"Why would you say that?" I ask.

"I need to know if I put you on this case, you aren't going to leave to go investigate Greg or run off to Iowa or find something else you need to chase. You need to be here, doing this."

My eyes narrow. "Is this about the case, or is this about Greg?"

He crosses his arms over his chest, his jaw squaring as he stares back at me.

"You were gone for a week," he says. "That sounds to me like a long time to watch security footage."

"Are you implying something?"

"I'm not implying anything. I'm saying maybe you aren't as separated from that life as you thought you were."

"That life?" I ask. "What's that supposed to mean?"

"When you said you were going to take a leave of absence and stay here, I thought that's really what you wanted," he says. "But then all it took was someone catching a glimpse of your ex-boyfriend, and you dropped everything to chase after him."

"I went back because the Bureau asked me to. And because I had to testify! Whether you're going to choose to understand it or not, it's not about any feelings I might have left for Greg. I want to know what happened to him. Anyone would. But maybe that's just not something you could ever understand."

I start out of the room, then stop and look back at him. "And just for your information, I did drop everything and come here for you."

I turn back to the door, but he reaches out to stop me.

"Emma, wait. I'm sorry."

I glare at him. Taking my sweet time.

"I appreciate you coming back here, and if you're willing to give it to me, I would like your help on the case," he finally admits.

I give a single nod, not trusting myself to say anything about what he said yet. "What do you have?"

He walks over to the table, and I follow him. He pulls a picture over and orients it in front of us, pointing down at the first image of Everly's body I've seen. In the picture, she's still hanging and most of the room is visible.

"Do you notice anything about the room?" he says.

"Not really. It looks perfect. No sign of a struggle."

"Exactly. Including," he runs his finger over the picture and points to the bed behind her, "the bed. If she climbed up onto the bed to put the rope over the ceiling fan and the noose over her head, she would at least mess up the comforter. But it's perfect."

"That's what you have? Evidence Maggie is a magnificent house-keeper?" I ask.

"You have such faith in me. No. That's just something that caught my attention. It got me thinking about the rope and how it was tied. Everly's ankles were tied together, and then the rope went around her neck. I had an expert in knots look at it, and he said there was no way she would be able to tie the knot she did around her own ankles, then also be able to do the rope around her neck. The positioning of the knots doesn't make sense. Someone else had to have tied them," he points out.

"Before they wrote the words on her," I say.

"What?"

"The words. They were written on her dress after the ropes were tied around her. Look, you can see where the marker rubbed against the rope right here, and where it says 'failure', the word is scrunched up, like its condensed, so it doesn't hit the rope. If the words were written before the ropes, they would be underneath them. She wouldn't tie herself up, then decide to write on herself."

"You've got a point. Add to that the coroner saying she didn't actually die from hanging, but from a separate strangulation, probably with a garotte, and you've got yourself a murder," he nods.

I let out a sigh and look at the pictures and papers in front of us.

"So... who do we look at first?"

CHAPTER TWENTY-SEVEN

ONE YEAR AGO

She hid behind the door, hoping no one would notice her standing there. She bided her time, listening carefully to what was happening on the other side of the door. She had to wait for the absolute perfect moment. If she went too fast, too soon, it would ruin everything. So, she waited. Tension built up in her stomach. Her heart started to beat faster. Finally, she heard the signal and burst through the door.

"Happy birthday!" she shouted along the dozen other waiters and waitresses flanking her.

The woman at the head of the table jumped in surprise and clapped her hands with delight at the cake held out to her. A single tall candle in the center of the cake glittered and sparkled, the flame shifting colors as it burned. Everyone sang, then cheered when the birthday girl blew out her candle.

"I'm just going to bring this back into the kitchen so we can slice it up, and we'll bring it out to you in a second," she said.

She grinned as she went back into the kitchen and set the cake down on the brushed metal counter. Taking a knife from the canister in front of her, she carefully started portioning the cake out onto a long row of small dessert plates they arranged ahead of time.

"You always seem so happy when people come in here to celebrate their birthdays," Lila said.

She grinned a little wider and shrugged.

"Birthdays are still kind of new to me," she said.

"You didn't celebrate your birthday when you were a little girl?" Lila asked.

She shook her head.

"Not really. My family isn't the kind for celebrations or anything frivolous."

"Yikes. They sound kind of awful."

"No," she shrugged, shaking her head as she tipped another slice of the tiramisu torte onto the next plate. "They weren't awful. Just strict and very traditional. I know they love me. They're just not particularly affectionate or demonstrative."

"But, let me guess, they were very good at making sure you got good grades," Lila teased.

"That they excelled at," she laughed.

"But you're an adult. No one ever threw you a party or anything?"

"I wasn't very social in high school or college. Then I lived with some people who didn't believe in any type of celebration at all, even holidays."

"Sounds like you haven't had the best experiences with roommates. Including your parents," Lila noted.

"That would be true. Which is why for the last couple of years, I've just been on my own."

She put the last slice of the cake onto the last plate and followed Lila out into the dining room. By the time she got to the table, everyone had already been served. The woman celebrating her birthday smiled at her.

"You enjoy that one!" she gushed. "Thank you for the surprise!"

She smiled and started back across the dining room to the kitchen. She glanced over her shoulder toward a voice that called out to her, and when she turned back around, she ran right into someone. A reflex had her grab for the cake, and her hand sank down into it.

"I am so sorry," she started.

"No, no. It's my fault."

She looked up and saw an incredibly handsome man smiling down at her. His dark eyes danced in his chiseled face, and the lightweight black sweater he wore accentuated wide shoulders and a broad, strong chest. His blond hair was a shocking contrast to the incredible darkness of his eyes, making them look infinitely deep, and she felt herself tumbling into them.

"I should have been watching where I was going," she said.

"I shouldn't have been walking right in front of you. I wasn't paying attention. Oh, look at your hand. You're covered in..."

"Tiramisu torte," she filled in.

"My favorite," he smiled. He swept his finger over the cream on her hand and tasted it. "Delicious."

She looked away to try to conceal the blush coming to her cheeks.

"I should probably get this into the kitchen. Enjoy your dinner."

She walked around him into the kitchen and set the plate down on the counter. Looking down at her hand covered in cream, she sighed and rolled her eyes, then went to the sink to wash it off. Clean again, she went back out into the dining room and found the man still standing where she left him.

"You left so fast I didn't even get a chance to introduce myself. Come here," he said. He led her over to a table near the front of the restaurant and gestured to another man.

"This is my brother Daniel. He's what distracted me and made me run into you. He must have mistaken you for our waitress because I know he would never be so rude as to shout at anyone who walked by just because he wanted water."

"Hello, Daniel," she said.

Daniel barely acknowledged her. She noticed the two men didn't look anything alike, but would never bring herself to ask about something like that.

"And this is Payton, and this is my daughter, Penelope. I'm Michael Blair. What's your name?"

Their eyes met, and she felt warmth spread through her in a way she never experienced.

"I'm Everly Zara."

CHAPTER TWENTY-EIGHT

NOW

"I don't understand," Michael Blair frowns. "You said it was a suicide. I've been believing that she killed herself, and now all of a sudden, you're calling it a murder? How does that even happen?"

"Sometimes the evidence isn't as clear as we'd like it to be," Sam explains. "A scene can look one way and lead to specific conclusions, then with further investigation, we find out it's different. It happens. It's unfortunate, and I'm sorry you have to go through this."

"I'm essentially having to find out the love of my life died twice. First, with the guilt and devastation of thinking she took her own life. Then I have to hear it again, only this time it's that someone took her from me in my own house. And I wasn't here to protect her. All this when I've just buried my two-year-old daughter. You couldn't possibly understand what that feels like," he says.

Sam shakes his head.

"No, I can't. And I'm not going to say that I can. But what I do understand is Everly deserves people to know what happened. She deserves justice. That's what we're trying to do for her. We just need to know what happened, and we can make sure she gets that."

Fighting tears, Michael throws up his hands and sits back on the couch for a second before leaning forward again towards Sam.

"What I need to do? Just tell me what I can do to help, and I'll do it," he says.

"We'll start with a few questions. Tell me again where you were the night before the morning Everly died," Sam says.

"I already told you. I was at my mountain cabin. It's a few hours from here, and the cell service isn't good. That's why nobody was able to get in touch with me."

"Was anybody with you at the cabin?" Sam asks.

"My daughter had just died, and people were blaming my wife, who I entrusted her to. Who do you possibly think I would have at the cabin with me?"

"I'm not trying to offend you," Sam protests softly, trying to calm him down. "I'm not making any judgments or assumptions. I just need to know the facts."

Michael rubs his hands over his face.

"You're right. I'm sorry. I'm just on edge."

"That's understandable," Sam nods.

"No, no one was with me. I went up there because I wanted some time to myself. I needed to think about everything that was happening and just get away from the chaos."

"Who was handling the final arrangements for Penelope?" I ask.

"No one at first," Michael says. "The sheriff here will tell you I was told they needed to keep her body for a few days for further investigation. I wasn't in a place where I could start thinking about a memorial service or anything like that. I wanted to talk to Payton before I did anything, and I just didn't want to talk to anybody."

"Did you do anything at the cabin that would record your presence there or prove how long you were there? Electronic locks, security cameras, anything like that?"

Michael gives a short laugh.

"Not at that cabin. It's not a mini-mansion tucked in the trees if that's what you're envisioning. It's fairly rustic. Just the basics. I did talk to a ranger the second day I was there. My land butts up against a park, and sometimes the rangers venture onto my property. I ran into one while I was out taking a walk, and I talked to him for maybe five minutes."

"Would that Ranger recognize you?" Sam asks.

"Absolutely. They all know me. His name is Jared Perkins," Michael says.

"Great. Just a couple of more questions."

Before Sam can say anything else, the door to the house swings open, and Daniel Blair stalks inside.

"Please tell me you aren't answering these people's questions without a lawyer here," he demands.

"I don't need a lawyer, Daniel," Michael says. "I don't have anything to hide. They're just asking me basic questions."

"Any time a cop asks you a question, you should have a lawyer with you," Daniel says.

"Is there a problem here?" Sam cuts in. "We're just asking questions."

Daniel rolls his eyes and looks back at his brother.

"Don't buy into the good old boy act, Michael. He's looking at you. You know it. Any time some woman gets herself killed, the first person they're going to look at is the guy she latched herself to."

"Don't talk about Everly that way," Michael snaps angrily.

"You don't need to try to protect her now, Michael. She pissed somebody off enough to make them kill her, and you're at the top of their list," Daniel says. He looks at Sam. "You need to leave. My brother isn't with proper counsel and won't be answering any more of your questions."

"Your brother is a full-grown adult and can make the decisions for himself," I point out.

"In all the time you're wasting standing around here asking him questions, you could be out finding the actual person who did this. Not that it bothers me too much that she's gone, but it seems to me you wouldn't want whoever it is getting into another one of these manors and doing it again," Daniel says.

"So, you think it was random," I raise an eyebrow. "A second ago you said it was because she pissed somebody off. Can't keep your story straight?"

"Back off," he says. "Everybody knows why you're here."

"Because I'm a hell of a good FBI agent?"

"Maybe you were once," he says.

"Come to think of it, since you're here, I have a few questions for you, too," Sam says. "Where were you the morning Everly died?"

"You've got to be kidding me. What reason would I have to kill her?"

"Oh, I don't know," I shrug. "You're just so warm and affectionate toward her. I can't imagine why anyone might suspect you'd like her gone."

"I didn't like the woman. I didn't think she was good enough for my brother, and then she killed my niece. That doesn't mean I would put my life at risk just to end hers. I needed to be here for Michael."

"So, where were you?" I ask.

"You seem to forget the idea of having a lawyer during questioning," he growls.

"This isn't an interrogation," Sam raises his hands in protest. "Just asking you a simple question."

Daniel sighs. "You know what? I'm in a magnanimous mood today. I'll help you along with your floundering investigation. I was at home."

"At home?" I ask. "That's your groundbreaking alibi? Was anybody there with you?"

"No, but Maggie knows I was there. She let herself into the house and went up to the bedroom. When she started screaming, I ran from my suite over to the main house. The medical examiner said she died just a short time before Maggie discovered her. That means I would have had to kill her, figure out how to lock the house from the inside, leave, run across the grounds without the gardeners seeing me, get back to my suite, and get in the shower. If you ask Maggie and the first responders, they'll tell you my hair was wet when they got there. Now, if you'll excuse me, I have business to attend to."

Daniel turns and stomps out of the house. Michael shakes his head.

"I'm sorry about him. Daniel has never been the friendliest of people, but he's my brother, and I've done as much as I can to take care of him. Life hasn't always been easy on him, and I've wanted to be there to make the rest of it better."

"Was it difficult between the two of you with him having so much contention toward Everly?" I ask.

"It wasn't easy," he admits. "He had something against her from the first night we met."

"He was there when you met?"

"I was out having dinner with Daniel, Payton, and Penelope. She was a waitress at the restaurant where we were eating."

His eyes mist over, and he looks into the distance like he's seeing that moment play out in front of him.

"I fell for her the second I saw her. She was incredible. I introduced her to everybody and hung around the restaurant until her shift was over. We talked for hours that night, then the next night I went in to see her again. We were together ever since. Daniel didn't take it well. He thought I should be getting more serious about settling down and looking for someone 'in my social class', as he put it. I didn't care about that. I liked hearing her laugh. I liked the stories she told and how full of life she was. When she started spending time with Penelope, she adored her. That sealed it for me. If my daughter didn't love a woman, there's no way I would be able to. But we both did."

"Just one more thing," Sam says. "The house was locked from the inside. All the windows and all the doors. Can you think of any way someone would be able to get in and out?"

Michael thinks about it for a few seconds, then shakes his head. "I have no idea."

Sam nods. "Thank you for your time. I'll let you know if there's anything else we need to know."

CHAPTER TWENTY-NINE

"There's something I still don't like about Daniel," Sam says.

We're back in the conference room bent over the pictures and evidence lined up on the table. I'm waiting for something to jump out at me.

"Sheriff?"

We both look up and see Savannah at the door.

"Yes?" Sam asks.

"They're here," she says.

"Great. Bring them back to the interview room. We'll be there in a minute," he nods. When the officer leaves, he looks at me. "I know your experience with Payton wasn't exactly pleasant. But I'm going to ask you to try to be gentle during this interview."

"What do you mean by that? I'm always tender and compassionate," I protest.

He looks at me, totally unconvinced.

"Emma. Don't be mean to her."

We head out of the conference room and into the interview room where Payton and Ian have been waiting, their chairs pressed close together as they hold hands between them. The interview room is an interesting tactic. Not all departments have one, but those that do tend to find them highly beneficial. As opposed to the stark coldness of an interrogation room, the interview rooms have some furniture, lamps for more comforting lighting, and sometimes even drink machines. They look more like a lounge or break room than somewhere you would be questioned by police. But that's the point. The room is meant to put you at ease and help you open up. It's especially effective at encouraging people who may feel defensive to talk more freely.

"It's good to see you two again," Sam starts. "I'm sorry it's in these circumstances."

"Why did you bring us in?" Ian asks.

"Did somebody actually murder Everly?" Payton asks.

She sounds like she's on the brink of tears, and I understand Sam's warning.

"Yes," Sam answers. "The evidence doesn't add up to her death being suicide. We've shifted the investigation to focus on finding the person responsible for her death."

"Then why do you have us here?" Ian asks again. "If you're trying to find whoever is responsible for killing Everly, why are you bothering to interview us again?"

"In a murder investigation, you start at the center," I explain. "If you don't have a clear and immediate idea of who committed the crime, you begin at the victim and move out like the ripples when you drop a pebble in the water. The closest people to Everly were Michael and her parents. We've already interviewed Michael, and her parents are planning on coming to town soon. Which brings us to the next ripple. The two of you."

"We're just gathering information," Sam adds. "The more information we have about all the people in her life, the easier it'll be to pinpoint changes or issues that might lead us to her killer."

"Payton, everyone says the two of you were on good terms. Especially considering the somewhat odd dynamic of your relationship," I say.

"I don't think it was odd. She was in love with the father of my child. It's as simple as that. We had no reason to not get along. In fact, she was a good friend. And an amazing influence for my daughter."

"Michael mentioned you were there the night he met Everly," Sam says. "But he didn't mention you, Ian."

"Ian and I hadn't met yet," Payton explains. "That night, I came by to spend some time with Penelope. Michael said he was hungry and had a craving for the stuffed shells at Angelo's. That was always one of our favorite places to go. He asked if we wanted to go with him, then invited Daniel to come along. It wasn't unusual for us to eat together or spend time at his house. As I'm sure you've heard, ours wasn't exactly the romance of the century. When it didn't make sense for us to be a couple anymore, we became friends and co-parents. It was an easy transition and wasn't made any more difficult when Everly came into the picture."

"How long was it after that before the two of you got together?" I ask.

Payton glances over at Ian, like looking at him will help jog her memory. "Not long. Maybe... three weeks? He joined my yoga class."

My eyes swing over to him. "Yoga?" I raise an eyebrow. "You don't really strike me as the namaste type."

"I hurt my back a few years ago, and it never fully healed. The doctor said yoga might help stretch it out and make my muscles stronger to reduce my pain," Ian shrugs.

Payton laughs softly. "But you're not wrong about your assessment of him. I think he lasted two classes."

"Just long enough to ask her out," Ian chuckles.

Payton leans into him, and Ian presses a kiss to her head.

"So, you really haven't been together that long," I say.

"What's that supposed to mean?" Ian asks.

"It's an observation. That's all."

"We were on a trip when she died," Payton offers as if she's trying to gloss over the discomfort. "When the doctors told us there was nothing else they could do for Penelope and she died, I couldn't think straight. I didn't know what to do. I just couldn't be around here anymore."

"Frankly, I was worried about what she was going to do to herself," Ian adds. "She was completely distraught, and I knew I needed to get her out of the situation just as she needed some time to process through it. Not that it was going to make it better, or she was just going to be able to move past it. But I thought getting away for a few days would clear her mind and help her over the initial shock."

"Where did you go?" Sam asks.

"A bed and breakfast in the country," Payton says.

"It actually, um... turned into our honeymoon," Ian says.

My mind goes blank. I couldn't possibly have heard what I think I just did.

"Your what?" I ask.

"Our honeymoon," Ian says again.

"You're married?" Sam asks in disbelief.

"Yes," Payton says, turning a teary-eyed smile toward Ian. "It wasn't planned or anything. It just happened."

"Why didn't you tell us? This is a murder investigation. You need to not keep things from us," I frown.

Payton looks at me strangely. "I wasn't trying to keep it from you. We just decided with all the turmoil going on, we would just keep it between us for a while. We didn't get married for anybody else. We got married because we wanted to."

"That close to your daughter's death?" I ask, a little more coldly than I mean to.

Her spine straightens, and she lifts her chin with indignance.

"I can't possibly expect someone with no children to understand, and I'll thank you not to judge my choice right to my face," she huffs.

"I'm not judging you. I'm trying to figure out what would possess you to do something like that," I say.

"Emma," Sam whispers, trying to quiet me.

"It's alright," Payton says. "I'm sure other people will ask. We might as well start explaining it now. I never thought I would be a mother. It's not something I ever wanted or envisioned for my future. But they say the universe has a way of working your life out for you and the way you're supposed to have it, not necessarily the way you think it should be. That's absolutely the case with Penelope. And when she came along, I discovered a love I couldn't even describe. Just because I am not equipped to be a full-time mother and would rather her be raised by a wealthy, privileged father who adored her and would give her anything doesn't mean I didn't love my daughter. I thought about her every day. I looked forward to every visit. When she... when she..."

Now the tears are starting to come back in her eyes, and some part of me feels bad for doubting her. I stuff it down. We still don't know who killed Penelope or Everly. For all I know, she's still a suspect, and I can't let myself get manipulated like this.

Ian offers her a tissue. She dabs her eyes and continues.

"When she died, it ripped a piece of me out. I've never experienced pain like that. And on top of the pain of losing my child, I had to deal with the guilt that she wasn't with me that night. I was out. I was just living my life. She was home with Everly. If I had been with her, she wouldn't be gone. Maybe if I spent more time with her or split custody or any of a thousand different things that went through my mind. I knew that day would, for the rest of my life, be excruciating. So, Ian offered an alternative. We got married in Penelope's honor. That way, every year, the pain of losing her would be softened by celebrating our anniversary. She would want us to be happy. To celebrate life and the future to come. Not waste any day in sadness."

CHAPTER THIRTY

I rest my elbows on the table in front of me and dig my fingers back through my hair. Exhaustion burns my eyes, but I'm not going to give in.

"I still say it doesn't make any sense," I say as Sam comes back into the conference room with a bag of Chinese food.

"Which part of it?" he asks, handing me a container of pepper steak and a pair of chopsticks.

"Any of it," I concede. "But especially them getting married. It's just really bothering me."

"Payton strikes me as a pretty impulsive person. I know couples who got married after a matter of weeks. It's not really that fast," he points out.

"It's not about it being fast," I say. "It's about it being on the day her daughter died. Within hours of finding out her toddler was dead, she was prancing up to the altar? Who does something like that?"

"You don't buy her explanation?" he asks.

"About trying to cover up the pain of her death with her wedding anniversary? Absolutely not. No mother would do something like that. She would want to spend that day every year memorializing her child, not drinking champagne and toasting to another year together. It just isn't right."

"I thought about you saying nobody knows how they're going to react to something until they go through it? Maybe this really is just her way of grieving," Sam says.

"No," I say. "I know what I said, and I believe that. But not about this. A mother that devastated about her child dying in mysterious circumstances doesn't just run off and get married. And that bullshit about her not wanting her to be sad and wanting her to celebrate life? Penelope was two years old. She's giving her the responsibility and thought processes of an adult. No. There's something else going on. We just have to figure out what."

I take a few bites of my food and realize Sam is staring at me. I look up at him with raised eyebrows.

"How did the investigation into Greg go?" he asks.

I sigh and shake my head. "I said we don't have to talk about that. That's not my investigation. I did my consulting, and it's done."

"But it's not done, Emma. You know that, and so do I. I overreacted, and I'm sorry. I just remember another time when you told me the FBI was just what you had to do, and you left Sherwood."

"I told you I was coming back this time," I protest.

"I know. But you still left to go search for an ex-boyfriend who is also in the Bureau and knew you in this whole new version of your life. I know it's pathetic, but I felt insecure. And it made me angry."

I reach out and run my hand down the side of his face.

"That's not pathetic. But it is way off base. I might have dated Greg during a time when you and I weren't in contact, and he might have been in the Bureau, but that doesn't mean anything. You still knew me well before he did and know me in a way he never did. And if I can take the liberty of stealing some of Bellamy's words, he was quite possibly the most boring FBI agent I ever knew. That doesn't mean I don't worry about him and wonder what happened."

"And you should. That would be something wrong with you if you didn't," he says.

"You don't need to be jealous. I promise," I smile softly. "Greg and I are over. That's ancient history."

A grateful look washes over him, but our moment is broken when someone knocks on the door.

"Come in," he calls, and I go back to my pepper steak.

Savannah's head pops into the room.

"There is someone here to speak with you, Sheriff," she says.

"When did you become my secretary?" he asks with a laugh.

Savannah rolls her eyes at him.

"I don't know, and I don't like it," she says.

We leave our food in the conference room and head out to the front of the station. An older man and woman huddle close together in front of the desk. When the man sees Sam, he takes a step toward him.

"Sheriff Johnson?" he asks

"Yes," Sam says.

"I'm Thomas, and this is my wife Greta. We are Everly's parents."

Sam nods as he shakes the man's hand.

"Yes. Thank you for coming. If you'll come into the back with me, we can talk. This is Emma. She's helping me with your daughter's case."

I greet both of them, and they nod back at me. When we get into the interview room, the couple opts to sit on the couch at the far end, perching close together at the edge of the center cushion. Sam and I move chairs closer.

"I'm sorry it took so long for us to get here," Thomas says.

"Please, don't worry. I can't even imagine how difficult this time is for you, Mr. Zara."

He shakes his head.

"Not Zara," he says. "Everly took that name when she was very young. It belonged to a family who helped my wife and I when we first came to this country, and who became very close with our daughter when she was born. You may call me Thomas."

"Did it bother you that your daughter changed her last name?" I ask.

"We came here so our children would have a chance at a life we never dreamed of, a life we never could have given them without being here. We had nothing at the time, but it was what gave us the strength and courage to make the move. We wanted everything for her. The best schools. The most opportunity. We didn't have much money, but we gave her everything we could to help her succeed and find her best life here. That included agreeing to a simpler last name that would help her feel more comfortable at school and meeting new people. It didn't feel like an insult. She still had her love for her family, and it was an honorable choice to choose the family that helped us so much," Thomas says.

He's doing everything he can to stay strong and fight tears pooling in his eyes. Beside him, his wife trembles, rocking back and forth as she cries.

"She was my only child," Greta suddenly starts. "My baby. And someone took her from us. Her past finally caught up with her."

My eyes jump over to Sam.

"What do you mean?" I ask.

"Greta," Thomas scolds under his breath, trying to quiet her, but she shakes her head adamantly at him.

"No," she says. "I won't stay quiet. Not now. Can't you see staying quiet has killed our child? We should have listened to her. We should have understood. But we didn't, and now she's gone."

Thomas stares into her face for several seconds, then finally nods.

"You're right. Tell them," he says. "Perhaps they can save another life."

Half an hour later, I pound on Michael Blair's door. It takes a few moments, but finally, he opens it.

"Emma, Sheriff," he says, confusion written on his face. "I wasn't expecting you. Did you find out something?"

"Yeah," I say, stepping into the house. "You could say that. Why didn't you tell us Everly was involved with a cult?"

He takes in a breath, his head hanging as he slowly closes the door. Gesturing ahead of him, he guides us into the living room where we can sit down.

"How did you find out?" Michael asks.

"Her parents came to the station," Sam says. "Her mother told us Everly started talking about a group she was involved with about five years ago."

Michael nods. "She met a guy in the coffee shop where she was working. He showed her a lot of attention and made her feel special, then invited her to meet some people he said were important to him."

"She told her parents they were impressed by her and wanted her to come study with them. That they were going to save the world. They thought she was talking about some sort of humanitarian program at first. Then she talked about them more and more, and said they wanted her to come stay with them."

He rubs his hands through his face, staring off as if he can see her alive still.

"Everly loved her parents. Very much. It was never lost on her how much they went through and sacrificed for her so she could have a life. So she could have a future. I think that's what convinced her to stay with the Society."

"What do you mean?" Sam asks.

"Like I said, she loved her parents. But they weren't affectionate. They weren't the type to lavish praise or give hugs. When she excelled at something, that was just her reaching her potential or doing what she was expected to do. They didn't see it as anything exceptional or worthy of acknowledgement. She got validation from them in other ways, but she still craved that sense of being cherished and appreciated and special just because she was who she was and not because of anything she was capable of accomplishing. These people knew that. The guy she got wrapped up with did everything he could to make her feel beautiful and precious. When he brought her to The Tower, the people there piled it on even more. They remarked on her beauty, they hugged her, they hung on her every word and were excited every time she came. They told her she was destined for greatness. Was one of the special chosen who would bring about the 'New Time', or whatever."

"And she fell into that?" Sam asks.

"Cults are incredibly powerful," I comment. "They exist because they appeal to what a person needs. A sense of community. A family. Respect. Wealth. Power. Feeling better than others. Feeling like they know something others don't, or that they will be privileged in some way over others. A promise of a better life. A sense of worth. They all do the same thing, just different packaging."

"Exactly," Michael nods. "They offered her so much and totally immersed her in this idea of an incredible future they were creating, by the time everything changed, she belonged to them. They erased her. From the first moment, they changed her name. Everyone within the Society was given a different name when they came. They were given roles and responsibilities. She didn't know at the beginning that her name meant she was chosen to be in the leader's harem. He convinced the women that having sex with him brought them closer to what he called The Essence."

"Their version of God?" Sam asks.

"He was their direct link to their version of God," Michael corrects. "Or something like that. They believed this man, Lucas, was going to bring about the cataclysmic reckoning of the Earth that would then allow their New Time to rise from the ashes. But in order to do that, he needed to... take advantage of them. The man who brought her in was a recruiter. He went out and found women to offer up to either become sex slaves, servants, or broodmares populating their new world. He found men to be either laborers, enforcers, or other recruiters."

"How long was she a part of it?" I ask.

"Two years. She was starved, beaten, raped, and worked brutally for the last six months of it before she managed to escape."

"That explains why her parents didn't hear from her," Sam muses.

"She wondered why they never did anything to try to find her," Michael says. "But even after she was out, they couldn't bring themselves to admit she was involved in something like that. They knew she got involved with something but would never admit it was as dangerous as it was. Even though she spent a year running from them."

My heart squeezes.

"Running?" I ask.

"She knew they were going to try to find her. People didn't just leave the Society. They would find her and bring her back. She didn't stay in one place for long, didn't socialize, was always on edge."

"And she just told you all this?" Sam asks.

"Yes. It wasn't easy for her. She was ashamed of what she went through and for being brainwashed by them. But I couldn't overlook the brand."

"The brand?" I ask. I suddenly realize what he's talking about. "The scar on her waist."

"Yes."

"It doesn't look like anything. There's no symbol or pattern in it," I point out.

"She dug the pattern out with a knife two months after escaping."

A shudder runs through me. That must have been extremely painful. It makes sense that if she was treated this horrifically, she'd want to destroy any part of their marking on her. You don't just dig out your own flesh to remove the mark of some normal organization you drifted away from.

"I still can't believe he didn't tell us," I tell Sam after Michael finishes up with us.

"He would have," Sam says. "I genuinely believe that."

"How are you so trusting?" I ask.

"Because I have to believe in the greater good of people. I couldn't deal with this job if I didn't. I have to believe he was protecting her. He said she was embarrassed talking about it, and I can imagine it was traumatic dealing with all of that. He wouldn't have wanted other people to know because he knows she wouldn't have wanted people to know. But I think eventually, the initial shock of her murder would have disappeared, and it would sink in just how important it was for us to know all the details."

"If he told us sooner, we could have investigated it sooner," I reply. "He said she knew people were after her. Think about her body. All those words written on it. The way it was strung up and bound after she was already dead. The fact that she was in her wedding dress. That's a message."

"And that's why we're going to visit the cult." He pauses. "That's not a sentence I ever figured I would have reason to say."

"Unfortunately, it's not the first time I've heard it," I tell him darkly.

CHAPTER THIRTY-ONE

The flight to Massachusetts takes only a couple of hours, and the proximity strikes me as we walk out into the parking lot to find our rental car.

"If she was running, why would she stay so close?" I ask.

"Sherwood isn't exactly a prominent place," he says. "Besides, Michael seems to feel like she wasn't afraid anymore once they got together. Maybe she didn't feel like they were chasing her anymore."

"It just feels so close. If she was truly afraid for her life, why wouldn't she go to the other side of the country? Or to another country. Why stay just a handful of states away?"

"Hiding in plain sight?" he asks. "We don't know why she made the decisions she did. That's why we're here. If we can find out what happened before she met Michael, we may be able to piece together how she died."

We drop our luggage off at the hotel and head for The Tower. It was surprisingly easy to find. We're able to just copy the address off a web listing. They call themselves The Society for the Betterment of the Future. It's oddly disorienting having them be so open. But at the same time, cults often masquerade as other causes or boldly advertise themselves as religions, self-help groups, or academic pursuits in an effort to both lure and deceive people.

There's no Tower visible as we drive up to the address listed. The entire property has a massive stone wall surrounding it, and a metal gate prevents access to the cobblestone road beyond. Sam drives into the entryway and reaches out to press an intercom button.

"Hello?" comes a voice almost instantly.

"Hi, my name is Sheriff Sam Johnson, and I'm here with Agent Emma Griffin of the FBI. We're looking into a missing persons case. Some of the information led us here, and we'd like the opportunity to talk to someone about it," he says.

"Absolutely, Sheriff. Come right in," the voice says pleasantly.

The intercom turns off, and I stare at him as the gate moves out of the way.

"We're lying to people now? That's an option?" I ask.

"It's not fully a lie. Everly's parents did, at one point, consider her a missing person," he offers. "Just consider it being undercover."

"I'm undercover as myself?" I ask.

"If that works for you."

As we drive up the cobblestone path, a building becomes visible in the distance. The slope of the landscape kept it out of sight, but as the path leads around in a wide arc, the stone structure rises up into view. Soon we come to a small building, and a young man steps out into our path. He gives a wave and a smile.

"Hello," he says. "Welcome. Continue along this path, and you'll find another guard. Tell them you are here to speak with Ruth, and they will allow you through."

"Ruth?" Sam asks. "We're here to speak to a man named Lucas."

The man looks like he is trying not to laugh.

"Oh, no. Lucas is not available for impromptu meetings. Ruth is his closest trustee. She will help you in any way she can."

I touch Sam's thigh to stop him from arguing, and the man steps back into the guard house. We continue driving, and Sam looks over at me.

"Michael said the leader is Lucas," he says. "Isn't that who we should speak to?"

"No. An organization like this rarely allows access to their leader. They will protect him at all costs. Besides, the leader doesn't usually do most of the orchestrating of the group. He is the one at the head, and he is worshipped as having absolute power and control. But the administration of his will is usually done by someone else. Not always, of course. There are some who do everything, but I doubt that's the way it is with this group. It's too sophisticated. Lucas is the leader and seen as their direct link to God. But I would venture to say Ruth is the one who oversees what's happening."

"So, Lucas is like the Queen," Sam says.

"You go ahead and refer to him that way. See how well it goes for you," I mutter.

We get through the second guard house and drive along the rest of the path to the back of The Tower. I see a row of cars parked several yards away, and Sam slides up into a space among them. By the time we get out and come around to the back of the car, an elegant-looking older woman is walking out of a door at the back of the building. She smiles and extends both her hands to us.

"Hello," she greets us warmly. "My name is Ruth. You must be Sheriff Johnson." She shakes his hand with both of hers. "And Agent Griffin."

She shakes mine, and we both nod our acknowledgment.

I pay close attention to our surroundings as she leads up through The Tower and into a lushly decorated room. Tall windows fill the space with bright light that illuminates white and pale floral furniture, vases of pristine white blooms, and silver trays of sweets on a highly polished table. There's the odd feeling they prepared for us even though they had only a matter of moments from the time we arrived at the front gate until now.

"Please, sit down. Make yourself comfortable. Priscilla makes the most incredible treats. Have some," she offers. "Can I get you a cup of tea?"

"No, thank you," I say.

"I'm fine, thanks," Sam says. "Since you knew our names, can I also assume you've been informed of why we're here?"

"Yes," Ruth says, her eyebrows suddenly knitting together in a concerned expression. "Benjamin tells me you're working on a missing persons case."

"We are," Sam nods. "And there are some indications this person has a connection to your organization."

She picks up a floral teapot sitting at the edge of the table and fills a cup with mint tea so strong I can smell it where I sit. She gives him a questioning look.

"A connection to us? I'm sorry, I'm not sure I understand."

I reach in my pocket and pull out my phone. Pulling up a picture of Everly, I turn the screen to face Ruth.

"Do you know this woman?" I ask.

Her eyes shine, and the smile returns to her lips.

"Sister Abigail," she says. "It's been so many years. She looks lovely."

"What did you call her?" I ask.

"Everyone who becomes a member of our organization is granted a new name for use within the group. It's a title of sorts. It helps to create unity and foster dedication to the organization."

"So, it's brainwashing," I comment brusquely.

Her head tilts to the side, but her smile doesn't falter.

"Of course not. Are you brainwashed by being called Agent? Or him by being called Sheriff? it's just a way for us to differentiate our lives within the Society and without."

"So, you do have lives outside of the organization?" Sam asks.

"If we want to," she says. "Nothing is keeping any of us here except our devotion to the cause."

"And what is that cause, exactly?" I ask.

"Just as our name says, we strive to improve ourselves and the world for the future to come. I'm sorry," she says, shaking her head. "I still don't think I understand why you're here. Has something happened to our Sister Abigail?"

"She told her parents she was spending time with someone associated with this organization. A few months later, they stopped hearing from her. We've heard she escaped after two years here," Sam says.

"Escaped?" Ruth raises an eyebrow. "There would be no need for her to escape. We're not holding anyone here. You won't even find locks on our doors. There's no need for them. The wall and the gate protect everyone within here. We're safe, so we can be free. Sister Abigail felt her time with us was done, so she left. It was that simple."

She's saying all the right things, and her tone of voice hasn't wavered, but I don't like this at all. I don't trust this Ruth, if that even is her name, as far as I can throw her.

"And if someone decides they don't like the type of freedom you're offering them?" I ask.

"Then they can go. It's their life, their future. We only want those who are truly committed to what we stand for and to the work we do. Holding anyone here against their will would be completely against our mission to foster love and beauty and create a new world of peace."

I notice stacks of photo albums lined up on a nearby table.

"Are those pictures?" I ask.

Ruth laughs. "Yes. Everyone says I am woefully old-fashioned, but I can't stand pictures being tracked on computers. Give me an actual photo album I can flip through any day."

"I know it's been several years, but do you think there any pictures of her in there?" Sam asks.

"Absolutely. She was deeply loved here."

"But you didn't keep in touch with her after she left?" I asked.

"We believe in separation from The Existence," she says.

"The Existence?" Sam asks.

"It's what we call the world beyond our society. We believe maintaining strong connections weakens our resolve and distracts us from the work we need to do. While our members are free to come and go as they please, we discourage them from maintaining attachments to The Existence. She chose to no longer be among us, so we had to let go of her."

I pick up a few of the albums and carry them back over to the sofa.

I flip through the pages until I see Everly's face smiling up at me. She's sitting at a desk, happily writing in a journal as other women do the same nearby. Another picture shows her baking a cake, while another is her lying in the grass laughing.

Ruth takes the book from my lap and gazes down at the pictures, stroking them fondly.

"She looks so happy. She always did. She thrived here and was doing such exceptional work. I don't think I'll ever understand why she wanted to leave."

"How about the man who introduced her to you?" I ask. "Is Jeremiah still a part of the Society?"

She looks at me questioningly.

"I'm sorry, but we don't have anyone by that name in the society."

"What?" Sam asks.

She shakes her head. "I know of every member who joins. I have been Lucas's most faithful follower and have personally seen to the guidance and protection of his flock for years. There has never been a Jeremiah."

I'm confused as I flip through a few more pages of the book. "Our witness told us the man who brought Everly into the... Society was named Jeremiah. He specifically told us before we came here. Everly told him that wasn't his name when they met, so it must be the one given to him by the Society."

I stop at two pages of pictures, capturing what looks like an elaborate garden party.

"What's this?" I asked.

"That is our annual Gathering of the Lights. It's a very important event for every member of our Society but especially our young women. If you look closely, I'm sure you'll see Sister Abigail."

I look at the date written at the bottom of the page. The span covers three days. The date in the middle is the day Everly died.

"Are the dates the same every year?" I ask.

"Yes," she tells me. "Those are very special dates for us, and Lucas hosts his garden party every year. Everyone within the Society is at The Tower for those three days. No one goes in or out. The fence stays closed to ensure we have the opportunity to celebrate the future to come without interference. This year's celebration was particularly beautiful."

"Can we have a tour of The Tower?" Sam asks.

"I can show you the common spaces," Ruth tells us. "But the rest is off-limits."

"Why?" I ask.

"We consider The Tower very much like a convent or monastery. There are spaces within it kept sacred just for our members. It's to protect the sanctity of our beliefs and the work we're doing. You are more than welcome to explore any of the common areas, but the living quarters, the devotional rooms, and Lucas's rooms are private."

Sam and I leave an hour later after venturing into every corner of The Tower she will allow us to. We stroll the grounds, visiting the garden depicted in the pictures. Nothing stands out to us. The people we meet look happy to be there and welcome us to return for another visit. I look over at Sam as soon as we get past the guard houses.

"I know he said Jeremiah," I say.

"That's what I heard, too," he confirms. "But she said there is no one named Jeremiah in the organization, and there weren't any pictures with captions that say Jeremiah or pictures of Everly with a man in any of those albums. Every member of the organization was accounted for at the time of the murder. They were all here for the festival."

"Is it possible she only told Michael she escaped from the Society?"

"Are you asking if I think she made it all up?" he asks.

"Not all of it," I muse. "Obviously, she was here and was part of the organization. We just don't know what happened to her from there."

"Do you have any FBI records that could shed more light on this place?" Sam asks.

"I could ask," I tell him. "Something tells me we won't find much of anything though."

"What do you mean?"

"All of this was so easy. She was very open to us and on the level. I don't deal with cults, but places like this are very careful and particular. They take advantage of every loophole they can get to keep out of trouble. We'd have to get enough evidence to get a warrant, which means opening up a whole case, which means telling Creagan what I'm up to if we wanted to do any further digging. And even then, if everyone involved is technically a consenting adult, there's little we can do without a lot more proof. We could spend all our time doing this and still end up in a dead-end."

"So we're back to square one, then?"

I let out a sigh.

"Back to square one."

CHAPTER THIRTY-TWO

TEN MONTHS AGO

She stepped into the bathroom and looked in the mirror, smoothing the wayward strands of hair back. She let out a breath and smiled at herself. It seemed like so long since she was able to truly smile that way. Maybe she'd never been able to. It was still hard to believe how much her life had changed. In just the last two months, her entire world shifted.

Because she met Michael.

She never imagined there were men in the world like him. Her father was a good man, a strong and responsible man who did what he needed to do to take care of his family. She had met several nice guys during her various stints at restaurants and bars, working however she could to keep herself afloat while drifting from place to place. But no one like Michael. He made her feel like she never had to drift again. He could protect her and take care of her. He could give her the kind of life she never would have been able to fathom. He could love her.

They were moving fast. There was no question about that, and she knew a lot of people disagreed with how they were handling their relationship. She saw the looks and heard the whispers, but she didn't let them affect her. It didn't matter what anybody else thought. All that mattered was what Michael saw when he looked at her.

Already she was living in his house. His breathtaking manor. It felt like the size of a small village back in her family's home country, and held the air of history and importance from the many decades it stood in the same spot. She knew he didn't always live here. His family hadn't owned the house for generations, and he didn't come from anywhere near as powerful a name as he had created for himself. That made this space all the more special because it was his. His and his precious little daughter, Penelope.

Everly adored that little girl. She had since the first moment she saw her. She was light and warmth and laughter packed into one small child, and it was hard to get enough of her. At nearly two years old, she already had a bigger personality than most of the adults she knew. She was dynamic, and Everly couldn't wait to watch the kind of person she would become.

Just thinking that way made her breathless. For the first time in her life, she could really look ahead and know what was waiting for her without having to be told. She knew it was Michael. In such a short time, he was already embedded in her heart, and she felt more alive and like herself than she ever had. It was like he discovered elements of her she didn't know existed until he was there to experience them. Maybe they didn't. Maybe there was only a piece of her there, and it required him to offer the other piece so both could come to life.

She took the pin from her hair and smoothed another section back, then secured the pin back in place. She patted her nose and cheeks to smooth her makeup and pressed her lips together to fix her lipstick. When she felt put together again, Everly walked out of the bathroom and down the hallway for the stairs. She was only halfway there when she heard footsteps behind her. It made her pulse quicken, a lingering effect of her time in The Tower that she had never shaken.

"Won't you just talk to me?" he asked.

She hated the sound of his voice. It burrowed itself in her ears and crawled down her spine. It made her hands sting and her stomach roll. But she wouldn't let herself show it. She didn't want to give him the satisfaction. He was doing this more frequently now, but if she didn't react strongly, it seemed to calm him in a way and shorten their interaction.

"I need to get back downstairs," she said.

"You should stay up here with me," he said.

"Please, stop," she said.

"Why? You know why I'm here," he told her.

"I need you to stop," she repeated. "This isn't going to change."

He drew in a breath, and she saw the muscles in the side of his neck twitching. He took a step toward her and lifted his hand like he wanted to run his fingers through her hair, but she recoiled from him.

"Why do you have to be this way? Can't you see this is inevitable? It has been since that very first day. It was me. It always was."

"No," she said. "I'm here to be with Michael. Nothing is going to change that. You just have to accept it. Please, step out of my way so I can go downstairs."

He hesitated, then reluctantly complied.

"I won't stop, you know. I've looked a long time for you. Now that I've found you, I can't let you go. You were meant to be mine."

CHAPTER THIRTY-THREE

NOW

The only way we could avoid having to go through at least two other airports before making it home was to take an absurdly early morning flight, so it's still early in the day when we finally get back to Sherwood. Sam is carrying my bag into the house when his phone rings. He pulls it out of his pocket and holds it to his ear.

"Hello? Sheriff Johnson speaking. Hi, Jared. Thanks for getting back to me."

He hits the speaker button, so I could listen to the conversation.

"No problem," says the park ranger Michael told us to contact. "What can I help you with?"

"I'm just checking up on a couple of things. Are you familiar with Michael Blair?" Sam asks.

"Very," Jared answers. "He's owned a cabin up here for years. He's always friendly when he comes up."

"Have you seen him recently?"

"Yes. Just a few weeks ago, actually. It was pretty devastating. He told me his daughter had been seriously hurt and had passed away. Michael looked so broken, like all the light and life had been taken out of him."

"So, he came up to the cabin after his daughter died?" Sam confirms.

"Yes. I thought it was a good idea for him to kind of get away and be able to mourn in his own way. I think he should have stayed longer."

Sam and I exchange glances.

"He didn't stay for long?" Sam asks.

"Not really. I actually didn't know he had left. I thought he was still up here in his cabin and just didn't want to talk to anybody. But there was a small forest fire. Nothing extremely serious, just a blaze caused by somebody's campfire not being put out correctly. It didn't take long for us to get it under control, but there was quite a bit of smoke, and the main road was blocked off for several hours. I went up to the cabin to check on him and make sure he was dealing with the smoke all right and didn't see any other signs of fire in his area. Even though it's private property and not technically part of the park, I try my best to keep an eye on it and look over the land when he's not around. Especially when it's something like a fire. The flames don't care who the land belongs to."

Sam dips his fingers into my pocket and pries out my phone. He quickly types something into the search bar.

"But anyway, he was gone. Haven't seen him since," Jared continues.

"Thank you so much, Jared. I really do appreciate you giving me a call back," Sam says.

"Absolutely. Anytime."

Sam hangs up the phone and turns to me. He holds up my phone, so I can see the screen.

"The fire was the night before Everly died," he points out. "There's no way Michael could have been at that cabin that morning."

"I think we need to pay Mr. Blair a visit," I say.

We arrive at the Blair Manor, and I notice Daniel standing on the porch. He comes down the steps toward us as we approach. His hands move constantly, anxiously adjusting the sleeves of a new shirt and tucking his bracelet out of sight.

"What are you doing here?" he asks. "We've gone over the requirement for my brother to have an attorney when you question him."

"And we've also gone over the fact that he's an adult, and he can make his own decisions. He doesn't need you to help him," I fire back.

"This investigation is a joke. I hope you know that. You haven't come up with a viable clue about anything, and all you're doing is harassing my brother, who is doing his best to grieve the loss of his daughter," Daniel says.

"And his wife," I point out.

Daniel's eyes burn into mine.

"We just found out your brother lied about his alibi. He doesn't have any proof of where he was the morning Everly died. We need to talk to him about that," Sam says.

"Well, he's not here. He's at the office today. It's the first time he's gone back to work since everything happened."

"Then I guess we'll drop by and wish him well for his first week," I say.

Wasting no time, we get back in the car, and Sam drives to Michael Blair's office. We go inside, walking right up to the reception desk.

"We need to speak to Mr. Blair," I say.

"Is he expecting you?" the receptionist asks.

"I highly doubt he is," I say. "But you can let him know that it's Sheriff Johnson and Agent Griffin."

She lifts a phone slowly to her face and mutters the information over the line. A few minutes later, the elevator doors across the lobby open, and Michael steps out, a concerned frown on his face. We meet in the middle of the lobby.

"What's going on here?" he asks. "You're coming to my work now?"

"Where were you when Everly died?" I ask, ignoring his protests.

"I already told you. Twice. I was at my cabin in the mountains, so I could have some time to think," he says. "I told you to call Jared Perkins if you needed some sort of confirmation."

"We did," I say. "And he had some interesting things to say about your visit. Like, did you know there was a forest fire the night before she died?"

Michael's eyes flicker over to the reception desk and then back to me.

"Come up to my office," he says.

The elevator ride up through the tall building is tense and uncomfortable. We make our way through the building and into a cavernous office that doesn't coincide with the personality I've known of him so far.

"Why did you lie to us?" Sam asks.

"I didn't lie to you," Michael says.

"Don't keep going," I tell him. "Jared Perkins had no idea you were supposed to be there for so long. Next time you want to create an alibi, at least make sure the person you're including in it knows what's going on. Because as far as he knew, you were just going through the worst time of your life and he thought you should stay at your cabin longer. You see, there was a fire that night before Everly died. Apparently just some campers who don't know how to put their fire out correctly, but it spread a bit and blew a lot of smoke toward your cabin. Perkins went by to check on you to make sure it wasn't bothering you and hadn't reached your property. Only you weren't there. That means you weren't at the cabin when she died. They set up roadblocks that kept anyone from traveling in or out of the area for almost two days."

"This is looking really bad for you," Sam adds. "You need to start telling the truth."

"Alright. I wasn't at the cabin, but I didn't hurt Everly."

"Where were you?" I ask.

"I can't tell you that," he says.

"I assure you, you can," I tell him, irritation flaring up now. "Because if you don't, things are just going to start looking a lot worse."

"I didn't hurt Everly. I loved her," he pleads.

"You have no idea how many times I've heard that," I say.

I turn away from the desk and start leaving his office. I have no more patience for this man.

"I'm being blackmailed," he finally blurts just before I get to the door.

That's something. Turning around slowly, I look at him through narrowed eyes.

"Excuse me?"

"I'm being blackmailed. That's why I didn't tell you where I actually was. The night before Everly died, I was supposed to make a payment to my blackmailer. So I went. It was late, and I didn't feel like driving all the way back to the cabin, so I stayed in a hotel. Paid cash. I ended up getting drunk out of my mind and staying there for the next day and night. When Everly died, I was blitzed and passed out in a cheap hotel by the side of the road."

"Who's blackmailing you?" I ask. "What are they blackmailing you about?"

"I don't know who it is. Every time I'm expected to make a payment, I get specific instructions, and I leave the money where I'm told. I've never seen anyone near it, and even when I've tried to hide and watch for it, I've never actually been able to catch anybody. Whoever it is, they're blackmailing me about Everly. Her involvement in the cult. They threatened to make her association with the cult and her escape public if I didn't pay them what they wanted, when they wanted it. I wanted to protect her, so I did it. She would have been humiliated and devastated if that came out. But it would also put her in danger. The people in the cult have threatened her and hunted her for years. Broadcasting that out to anyone who would listen would just be putting her up for sacrifice."

"Can you prove what you're telling us?" Sam asks.

"Of course. Everything is at my house. I can bring you there right now."

CHAPTER THIRTY-FOUR

R ather than going through the ornate front door of Michael's massive manor like we usually do, he leads us around to the back and a private entrance. We pass through a narrow white gate into a tiny courtyard that reminds me of The Secret Garden. From there, we go to a door with a small keypad beside it. He pushes aside a protective shield that covers the buttons and types in a code. The lock within the door clicks, and Michael pushes the door open.

"Do you get into the house like that often?" I ask as we step inside.

"Not really. Just when I'm specifically headed for my office or library. Usually I go to the front door."

"But you do sometimes use this door. Like more than just every few months?" I ask.

"I suppose. It's the one really fancy piece of technology I had added into the house other than the security cameras. When I first bought this house, I fell in love with the original woodwork and doorknobs and fixtures. All those little details you don't think you will ever care about until you find a house you want to be in forever. Then all of a sudden, those details matter a lot. I happen to love the doorknob on this door. The only problem is, they used a very specific, very old key that was probably lost fifty years ago. There was no way to retrofit a key lock onto the door. So, in order to preserve the structure of the door and the doorknobs, I had it outfitted with an electronic lock. It only needed a few minor adjustments, and now all I have to do is put the code in and the magnets inside the door holding it closed release.

"Who else knows about this door?" I ask.

"Nobody that I know of," he says. "People don't go past the fence into the courtyard, and the area of the house this door leads into is my personal space. Not even Maggie goes in there. Why?"

"This is how Everly's killer got in and out of the house," I tell him. "Think about it. It's not covered by the surveillance cameras, so there would be no record of anybody going in or out of it. You don't have to use a key, so there's no visual indication of a door being broken into. When the crime scene investigators toured the house to make sure it was locked up, all they had to do is turn the doorknob, and it would be locked. Because there's an antique keyhole on the interior of the door, it looks like it has to be locked from the inside, that there's no way someone could go outside and secure the door properly. But that's not the case."

"But nobody knows my code," Michael argues.

As soon as the words are out of his mouth, a crash at the end of the hall sends us running.

We dart down the hallway towards the sound. He opens a set of arched double doors into an impressive library, where somebody already seems to be catching up on their reading material. I walk up to Payton and hold my hand out for the folder she's gripping. She offers it over, and I take it from her hand.

"A little bit of light beach reading for your upcoming vacation?" I ask.

"Payton, what are you doing?" Michael asks.

I hand the folder over to him, and he looks down at it.

"This is my life insurance information," he frowns. "And my monthly accounting."

"Michael, please," Payton pleads, coming toward him. "It's not what it looks like."

"Really? Because it sure as hell looks like you broke into my house to steal personal information," he snaps.

"I just wanted to check it," she says.

"Why?" Michael asks. "Why would you need to go through my financial information?"

"Because she wants to make sure she's still set," I point out. "Even though you had full custody of Penelope, you still send her money every month, didn't you? You call that child support, but it really was just taking care of her."

"Yes," Michael says. "There was a time when I really cared about her, and she is the mother of my child. I wanted to make sure she was alright. And, frankly, there were times when I knew she wasn't. So, I started giving her money every month."

I turn my gaze to Payton directly.

"But now that there's no child, you started to worry about those monthly payments, didn't you? You relied on them and wondered if there was any way he was going to continue to give you that money. The loss of your daughter meant the loss of your income as well. But, on the other hand, maybe not. Like he just said, he cared about you. And the two of you had gotten to be even closer friends while raising Penelope, so maybe he would keep supporting you. There's only one thing standing in the way. A wife. How many women do you know who would feel comfortable with their husbands shelling money out to their ex-girlfriend every month? As soon as he married Everly, you knew it was only a matter of time before your support from him was gone."

"No," Payton says, shaking her head to try to will away the tears. "I didn't do anything to Everly. I wouldn't hurt her. Everly was my friend."

"Babe, what's going on?" Ian asks as he comes through the door, then stops in his tracks and looks at us.

Payton rushes toward him.

"They think I murdered Everly," she says, her voice cracking. "They think I did it so Michael will keep giving me money."

"That's ridiculous," Ian scoffs.

"Is it?" I ask. "What do you do for a living, Ian? I don't think I've ever heard."

"What's it to you?" he asks, holding his arms around Payton like he's protecting her from me.

"Because it seems to me a man without a job or with a steady but low paying job would find it extremely appealing to have a girlfriend with a steady income stream from a multimillionaire."

"I've never had money," Payton says. "So it didn't really matter to me that much. Yes, it was nice to have and to not have to worry, but I wouldn't kill my friend over it."

"Not even if that friend is also responsible for your daughter's death?" Sam asks.

Payton pulls away from Ian and reaches into her pocket for her phone. She sweeps the screen open and sweeps through it for a few moments before turning it around so I can look at it. It's an image of her and Everly together. They're wearing bikini tops and cut off jean shorts and sitting on what looks like a blanket on the sand. I stare at the image intently, trying to retain as many of the details as possible.

"Look. She was my friend. Somebody I cared about and trusted. Of course, I was devastated when Penelope died, and I felt betrayed, but I didn't hurt her. It would have been another betrayal. A betrayal of my daughter, who loved Everly," Payton says.

"So, explain the aggression over the department dropping the criminal investigation into Penelope's death. Without that investigation, you would have been able to hold Everly, and by extension, Michael, accountable for your child's death. Just another income stream gone," I point out.

"I wanted her to face justice," Ian says. "I don't know if she purposely hurt her or if it was just an accident, but she's dead because of her. And I wanted to know she wasn't just going to be pushed under the rug."

Michael steps up close to Ian and points toward the office door.

"Get out," he growls through gritted teeth. His eyes move over to Payton. "Both of you."

"Michael," Payton gasps.

"Now."

They start toward the door, and Ian turns around to look directly into my eyes.

"The Heather Branch Inn," he says.

"Excuse me?" I ask.

"That's where we stayed on our honeymoon. The Heather Branch Inn. You can check."

He stomps out of the room, and soon, we hear the front door slam.

"I'm sorry, Michael," Sam says.

"At least Emma figured it out before I lost a lot more than I already have," he says.

"I'm not done yet," I say. "We still have to ensure Everly's killer doesn't get away with it."

"Do you really think Payton killed her?" Michael asks.

"No," I tell him. "It doesn't fit her personality. She is far too care-free to do something that complex."

"So, that's it. We have nowhere else to go," Michael says.

"Not quite. There's someone else I want a word with. But this one I need to do on my own. Michael, why don't you file a report with Sam? Documenting her coming into the house is important. Even if she didn't take anything, it's important to show intent and ability," I suggest.

"Where are you going?" Sam asks.

"Not far," I tell him. "I'll let you know when I'm ready."

CHAPTER THIRTY-FIVE

THREE MONTHS AGO

"**D**on't do this," he pleaded. "Please, don't do this."

Everly squeezed her eyes closed and tightened her grip on the edge of the bathroom sink.

"Stop," she said. "I can't have this conversation again. I need you to stop doing this."

"You can't honestly be happy with him. What do the two of you have in common? What do you enjoy about each other?"

"I am so happy with him. I don't know what else to tell you or how else to explain it to you. I know you're unhappy, but that's not my fault. I can't be responsible for that."

"How can you say that?" he snapped. "You're responsible for all of this. Who else could possibly take the blame?"

"There's no blaming. Nobody did anything wrong. All I did was fall in love," she said in exasperation.

"This is the wrong person. It should have been with me. And you know it just as well as I do. We fit so much better together. Can't you feel what happens when we're in the same space? Can't you feel the spark? The energy? It's been there since the very first time I saw you. I know you feel the same way."

"I don't. I'm in love with Michael. He asked me to marry him, and I accepted. Our reception is in less than an hour. Today should be one of the happiest days of my life. Please don't keep doing this to me. I need you to accept that I married him, and it's not because he asked first, or he somehow manipulated me. I married Michael because I love him, and he's who I want to spend the rest of my life with. Nothing can compare to what he and I have. And I'm not going to leave him for anyone."

"How can you even say that? You don't know. We have no idea how incredible we would be together. You won't even let me touch you," he said.

He took a step closer to her, and Everly withdrew slightly. She watched him rove his eyes over her face and along her neck. His hand lifted and touched her cheek, then stroked back through her thick hair. He let out a long breath.

"You can't tell me you don't feel that," he said.

Suddenly, he turned her around, and his body pressed against her. She could feel each of his breaths rising and falling raggedly against her chest. His face came close to hers, so close, the tip of his nose brushed against her, and she could feel the warmth of his breath. Just as suddenly as it happened, it stopped. He stepped back.

"Don't ever touch me again," she spit.

"I won't ever stop trying."

He walked away, and she sagged against the counter, willing the tears to stay in her eyes. She would be celebrating her elopement to Michael soon, and she didn't want anything to spoil it. Everly smoothed her hair into place and checked the outfit she chose in the mirror. She walked out of the room, and after a few seconds, heard someone walking up behind her. She whipped around, and a scream tore out of her as hands came for her throat.

Before he could squeeze too tight, the sound of a door shutting catches his attention. "This isn't over," he growls in her ear.

She sagged on the step below her. Maybe she wasn't as safe with Michael as she thought.

CHAPTER THIRTY-SIX

NOW

"Where did you get your bracelet?" I ask.

Daniel looks at me from his open front door and rolls his eyes.

"Did you get your fill of harassing my brother and so now you've come here to talk fashion with me?" he asks.

"I'm just curious. It's unusual. Where did you get it?"

Daniel looks at his wrist and twists the gold chain around a few times.

"I don't remember. I've had it for years. It's just a bracelet," he shrugs.

"I don't think so," I say. "I don't think you've had it for years at all. I think you had it for a few weeks. Just tell me. Did you take it off of Everly, or was it sitting on her dresser?"

"What are you getting at?" Daniel asks.

"It's her bracelet, isn't it? Don't try to lie about it. Payton showed me a picture of the two of them together earlier, and Everly was wearing that bracelet in the picture. I remember I've seen several other pictures of her wearing that bracelet. Now, suddenly you're wearing it."

Daniel's head falls back, and he shifts uncomfortably. Suddenly he looks at me with an intense look in his eyes.

"I didn't hurt her. I would never do anything to hurt Everly," he insists.

"Because you loved her," I say. "Didn't you? It drove you insane every day to watch her with your brother. You wanted her for yourself from the first moment you met her. It was the same night you met her. But he saw her first."

"No, he didn't," Daniel says. "I saw her first. We were sitting at a table at the front of the restaurant, and a woman a few tables away was celebrating her birthday. When the kitchen door popped open, and a dozen waiters and waitresses came swarming out to present her cake, I couldn't help but look over. It was a bit of a spectacle. That's when I saw her. She was standing there holding the cake, and the candle lit up her face. I could have sworn she looked over at me. Even for a second. I pointed her out to Michael, and of course, he couldn't let well enough alone. He had to get up and go try to find out more about her. She came back out of the kitchen with a slice of cake, but I saw Michael coming toward her, and I called out to him. She turned to look at me and then ran into him."

"Do you think he did it on purpose?" I ask.

"I don't know. But I know he brought her over and told her I was trying to get her attention rather than our waitress. He thinks things like that are funny. He's always done things like that. Ever since we were kids. She was even more beautiful up close. I wanted more than anything to ask her out. I'm the one that pointed her out to Michael, so he had to know I was interested in her. But he swooped right in. I didn't even have a chance."

"Is that why you acted like you hated her?" I ask.

"I wasn't acting. In a lot of ways, I did hate her. I hated her for being as incredible as she was and not realizing it. I hated her for the way she looked at Michael and the way she didn't look at me. I hated her for her strength and courage to drag herself out of situations she was in when she was younger. That's the type of strength and courage I don't have. I've spent my entire life riding my brother's coattails because he'll let me. Our parents call me their son and say they love me just the same as Michael, but I know it isn't true. I've never felt adequate. I've never felt like I measured up to him. He has always been smarter, stronger, braver, more creative, funnier... any adjective you could come up with, that was my big brother. But he let me cling to him and benefit from all those things. When I met Everly, I thought maybe for once, my luck was going to change. She was going to be my bright spot and finally put me in front of my brother. But it didn't happen," he mutters.

"But you couldn't bring yourself to leave the in-law suite," I say. "No matter how much you pretended to hate her, no matter how much you say you actually did, you couldn't actually bring yourself to leave. You wanted to be closer to her to still get to interact with her on a regular basis. But it wasn't working the way you wanted it to. So, you started blackmailing your brother."

Daniel's eyes widen. "How did you know about that?"

"Michael told us. When he was describing what the blackmailer said and the things he threatened, then I noticed the bracelet, and I figured it had to be you. Everly was deeply embarrassed about her involvement with the cult and what she went through. He wouldn't tell just anybody. But he would tell you, his brother. I'm assuming you used your imagination to fill in a few extra embellishments, so he didn't put it together. He doesn't know it's you. I don't think he needs to know it's you. His blackmailer can just drift off into the ether, and the money can make its way back into your brother's bank account."

"Thank you," he says.

"I just want to know why you would do that. You scared him. You upset him. What was the point?"

"That was the point. I wanted to scare and upset him. I wanted him to get tired of it and decide it wasn't worth dealing with anymore. When Penelope died..."

He draws in a trembling breath and hits his head back against the door frame, letting his body slide down to sit on the floor. "When she died, I didn't have anything left. That little girl was my heart. I didn't grow up to be much. Having her around and being able to influence her made me feel like maybe I had another chance. I could still put something good into the world. Then she was gone, and there was nothing left. I had to try with Everly. The morning she died, I gathered up all the evidence about the blackmail and went over to the main house. I knew Michael still hadn't come home because I sent him on another drop. It was breaking my heart to see her that way. I laid it all out for her. I told her how much I loved her and wanted to be with her. Then I told her I had been blackmailing Michael. He hadn't told her and had made no move to stop it. I told her that showed the type of man he was, dishonest and ashamed of her. I told her I would never be ashamed of her, and I thought she was the most incredible woman I had ever met."

"But it didn't work," I say.

"She said Michael not telling anybody about the blackmailing wasn't weak or him trying to hide. It was him protecting her, showing her how much he loved her. Then she asked why I never tried with Payton."

"Payton?" I ask, surprised by the detail.

"We got close after Penelope was born. I don't think a lot of people realized that because they were so fixated on her being my brother's ex and still spending time with all of us. Somehow his money and prominence make it so a perfectly normal arrangement for anyone else is bizarre for him. But she and I did spend a lot of time together. Sometimes she would come hang out at my place if Michael was out. But it never turned into anything. I didn't want it to. I guess that's why it hurt so much when Everly suggested it."

"And when you left, she was fine?" I ask.

"Perfectly. I told her I would never forget her and took the bracelet. She didn't argue with me. I felt like that was us coming to an agreement in a way. We'd always know, but it didn't have to be talked about. Then I left. I spent the rest of the morning sitting under a hot shower until I heard Maggie screaming."

"You've managed to be really cold and even callous about her. You even stayed with her body. How could you do that?" I ask.

"Because I thought she killed herself, and it destroyed me. It was easier to slip back into hating her than it was to actually feel it. Then when Sheriff Johnson announced it was now considered murder, I hated myself for leaving her even more. If I'd been there for just a little longer, I could have protected her," he says.

"Just one more question. When you went to see Everly, where was she?"

"Where was she?" he asks.

"In the house. Where was she?"

"The sink and changing area of the bathroom," he says. "I came through the connection between the two houses. Most people don't even realize it's there. Michael had the door concealed when he first bought the house, so it didn't look strange."

"Where is it?" I ask.

"At the end of the hall beside the bath. It's hidden inside a wardrobe cabinet. The back panel moves out of the way. It's easier to use that than the doors, but Michael hates it. I don't do it often, and we've never told anybody they're there."

"Thank you, Daniel. I truly am so sorry for your loss."

"Thank you," he says weakly, looking down between his pulled-up thighs at the porch. "You know what moment of that morning will always stick with me?"

"What?" I ask.

"When I saw her hanging there and saw the scar on her hand, all I wanted to do was hold it. I don't think I'll ever be able to get that out of my mind."

"Scar on her hand?" I raise an eyebrow.

"You didn't notice? Everly had a scar on her pointer finger. She told Michael the branding on her waist wasn't the only way to mark the women. They were also required to wear metal bands on their pointer finger to mark them. At first, it seemed like a gift. Then they start heating it with coals and the branding iron. Hers left her with a deep scar."

That makes something course through my head.

"Son of a bitch."

CHAPTER THIRTY-SEVEN

HIM

"I want answers," he demanded, hovering over the two men.

They cowered in front of him. Exactly how he wanted them. Both were shirtless, putting their tattoos on full display. The massive sea monsters carved deep into their backs and filled with black ink marked them as loyal to Leviathan. He had a similar tattoo, but the waves etched beneath its undulating body were tinged with red, signifying the blood that brought him to his place as head of the organization.

"We don't know," one of the men answered.

"Neither of you?" he asked.

"No," the other replied. "We don't know who supplied the explosives or planted them."

"And you haven't heard anything?" he asked.

"Nothing," the first man answered. "We've asked, but no one is talking. Most who know assume it was Leviathan."

That number would amount to little more than a handful. Those who knew about Leviathan pledged their lives to the organization. They were recruited from the streets, brought in fresh from the prisons, courted from universities and government agencies. Among them, the most brilliant and skilled scientists and craftsmen to create weapons and implements of warfare, the well-connected to find supplies and dedicated clients, and the reckless and driven to take the biggest risks.

Those who knew Leviathan existed but who were not counted among its number were very few. To know about the organization was a burden, and a privilege, for Leviathan was created for chaos. Its goal was to nurture fear and foster warfare. When society became too balanced, it stagnated. Chaos allowed for that imbalance. A terrorist organization so sleek and expertly run it had not even been identified by the CIA, Leviathan lived up to its name.

For thirty years now, he had given of himself fully. He unleashed death, destruction, and turmoil onto an unsuspecting world. And with that came power and a constant stream of money from the terrified arming themselves for war. In those thirty years, he rose through the ranks, gaining influence and dominance until the blood was etched into his back, and he took full control.

The chaos kept people aware of the moment and didn't allow them to forget to live. Because at any second, the option may no longer be theirs.

But despite the credit being given to them in whispers among the select few in the know, this time it wasn't them releasing torment. The explosion at the bus station wasn't his plan, and it infuriated him that someone else orchestrated it.

"Do any of you understand the sheer magnitude of the situation? Do you grasp the severity of what happened?"

"Yes," both men answered.

"I don't think you do. I don't think either of you could possibly appreciate just how disastrous this really was. I don't care about the deaths. The destruction means nothing to me. It was just another building. But he was in there. And what if it had been Emma? If she was there…"

He drew in a breath to quiet his mind and stop the sentence from forming. He couldn't even bring himself to imagine the consequences if Emma had been in that bus station. The effects of the explosion were already impacting his plans. Everything had been laid out exactly as it should have been. They had timed every step, prepared for what they believed was every eventuality. It never even occurred to him that someone else's eyes would be on that station.

Now he had to know who. The vast majority of the weapons in Virginia and several surrounding states were run through him. Men scattered across the country and across the globe prepared to go to battle armed with artillery he provided. Whether it was gang members facing off with handguns in battles over street corners and drugs, or small armies tired of seeing the blood on the sand, he provided a service to them. He ensured they had what they needed to further his goals, in exchange for exorbitant fees and loyalty.

The favors owed to him by those who took patronage of his empire collected like the money in his bank account. He kept them close, rarely calling them in. It was better to have these people beholden to him and prepared to do whatever he asked of them than it was to make a simple task simpler. But now it may be time to start cashing in some of that debt.

"I want to know who supplied those explosives and why they planted them. And I want them brought to me."

"Brought to you?"

"The plans must change. There's too much danger. I've already had to spend so many years away from her. I've done my time. I can't be without her anymore. Soon it will be time. And nothing will stand in my way."

CHAPTER THIRTY-EIGHT

"Did you find those pictures?" I ask as Sam comes into the house.

"Most of them. I can pull up more on the computer. Care to tell me what's going on?" he asks.

"Just bring them over here. I need to look before I can be sure," I tell him.

He obliges, and I kneel down on the floor beside the coffee table to get a better view of the pictures he spreads out in front of me. They are enlarged glossy versions of crime scene pictures and autopsies. I arrange them carefully and scan each, taking in every detail.

"All of these are from Massachusetts and Connecticut," he points out.

"I know. Can you pull up the other ones I asked for?" I rearrange the pictures. "A few years ago, we looked into a case, but it never really pieced itself together. There wasn't much to go on, and the only real reason they called the Bureau in was because it crossed state lines."

"But nothing ever came of it?" Sam asks.

"No," I shake my head. "It's technically still under investigation, but it's long cold."

"Why do I get the feeling you're warming it right up?"

"That's what I'm going for."

"What was the case?" he asks.

"Over the course of about two months, eleven bodies were found scattered across a fairly small area straddling Massachusetts and Connecticut. They were all in similar stages of decomposition, with some variation based on where exactly they were found, how much was exposed, and other factors. But it was enough to make the determination they were all killed and left in the area within a very short time of each other, possibly even at the same time."

"Eleven murder victims at the same time?" Sam asks. "A spree killer?"

"That was our initial thought. Until we really started looking at the victims. These victims," I point at the pictures on the table in front of us, "I didn't think it would be too hard to find the killer. It was a case we definitely tried not to sensationalize. We kept media down as much as we could and limited news exposure. With something like this, you can never know who might be inspired by it. Keeping our investigation under wraps also meant fewer gawkers at the burial site. But it's impossible to keep something of this magnitude completely hidden. Crime scene photos leaked and autopsy reports ended up on the news. It was a disaster."

"I can't remember hearing anything about something like that," he muses.

I nod. "You probably did, you just aren't connecting it. It was managed. Usually presented as a 'mass grave with an indeterminate number of bodies' or as several different cases. But the investigation stalled. We couldn't make any connections between the victims or figure out how they got there. It was very clear they were all linked. Each of the eleven victims was male, within ten years of each other in age, and extremely similar physical features and proportions."

"Like eleven versions of the same person."

"Something like that," I answer.

"If you already worked on this case, why didn't you just ask the Bureau for the case files?" Sam asks.

"I don't want to get them involved just yet. Besides, this case is a sticking point for Creagan. He doesn't like anything marring his record. Multiple unsolved murders is definitely not something he appreciates. If he knew I was looking into it again, he'd be furious. So, for now, it's leaked scans and public access documents. Not ideal, but they work," I say.

"What happened to the victims?" he asks.

"They all showed signs of being starved, beaten, and put through extreme physical exertion in the months leading up to their deaths. A few of them seemed to have died from those factors. Others were shot in the base of the skull."

"They were executed."

I nod. "Like they all outlived their usefulness at the same time. There was one other thing they all shared." I pick up two images. One is from the crime scene where the man's body sprawled in the dirt, barely covered with branches. The other was from an autopsy of another of the men. "Look at their wrists. Do you see the scars?"

"It looks like they were bound with something," Sam squints.

"That's what it seemed like at first, but looking at the scars further, we found out they were actually burns. The characteristics of them suggested hot metal."

"Handcuffs?" Sam asks.

"Since each of the men only had one scar, it seemed much more likely it was a bracelet. There was tremendous breakdown of the skin around the scars, but on one of the victims, the burn had a symbol in it. It didn't match anything in any of our databases, and we could never find who it belonged to."

I lift my eyes to Sam and see the realization form in his gaze.

"First thing in the morning, I'll make some calls, start forming a team," he says. "We don't have a task force equipped to handle something like this, but we'll reach out to the departments in the area and see what they can provide. It isn't our jurisdiction..."

"No, it isn't," I interrupt. "This case just blew open and no offense, but you have nowhere near the resources you'll need."

"So what do we do?"

I give a heavy sigh and rub my fingers on the bridge of my nose.

"I'll call Eric," I finally say. "I really don't want to talk to Creagan right now, but this is way above us at this point."

Sam nods and starts helping me pick up the pictures. I've gathered up a big stack in my hand when I notice something on the floor under the edge of the couch.

"What's that?" Sam asks.

I stare at it, baffled by what I'm seeing.

"It's my father's birth certificate from the midwife in Iowa," I tell him.

"See? It wasn't actually missing. It must have just fallen on the floor and got kicked under the couch," he says.

I shake my head. "I looked under there. Several times. It wasn't there."

"Well, it must have been, because there it is."

"No, Sam, something's different about it."

"What do you mean something's different about it?" he asks.

"Look." I climb to my feet and hold it out to him. "Remember the 'X' that wasn't in either single or multiple births? It moved."

"Things don't just move on forms, Emma," he says.

"It's not in the same spot. The 'X' was close to the multiple birth box and even had one of its legs in that box. Remember? We had a whole discussion about it. Now it's in the middle, not touching the box at all."

"You must be remembering wrong," he says.

I take out my phone and search through the gallery until I find the picture I took of the form.

"This is the original," I tell him, showing him my phone. "This one has been altered." I look at the paper in my hand, more carefully. "I need to go back to the storage unit."

"Now?" he asks. "What about the case?"

"Yes, now. I need to see what's in the other boxes and then go through the pictures I put in the attic. We can't do anything about the rest of this until tomorrow. I'll call Eric on the way."

"Alright. Let's go."

I hang up the phone, just having sent the last of all the information we have in an email. I know Creagan will probably round on me when he finds out I've been working on this, but hopefully, the idea of finally solving his long-cold case will soften his heart. Maybe. I'm not actually sure Creagan even has a heart.

But there's not much else I can do about it right now, so I try to shake it all out of my mind and focus on what's ahead. The storage unit. My father's birth certificate. Funny how every time I try to just relax and get away, I find myself in some other crazy situation.

As we drive toward the storage unit, a strange feeling creeps up my back. I glance in the rearview mirror a few times before Sam looks over at me.

"What's wrong?" he asks.

"I think there's a car following us," I tell him. "It's been trailing us since we turned onto the main street from the house."

He looks behind us, and the headlights start sinking back.

"Keep an eye on them."

I watch through the mirror for the rest of the drive. For the next few minutes, the car varies its distance from us, getting closer for several seconds, then falling back. I can't see what type of car it is because of the glare of the headlights. We're almost to the storage unit when the car hesitates, then turns onto a residential street.

"They turned," I say.

"Just try to calm down," Sam says. "You're getting too worked up."

"Let's just get the boxes and go back to my house."

We go through the gate and to the back of the parking lot. The tall light posts create their pools of light on the pavement but don't offer much else. Sam goes to open the door to the unit as I walk around to open the trunk. Seconds later, I hear a crash and the sound of metal grinding against pavement.

"What the hell was that?" Sam asks.

He starts running toward the entrance moments before headlights slice around the corner. The mangled front gate clings to the hood as the car speeds toward us. Sam tries to get out of the way, but he doesn't have a chance.

He crashes hard against it. His body bounces over the fence, slides across the windshield, and lands in a heap on the ground.

I scream and jump into the car behind the wheel. There are no keys. Sam has them.

An instant later, a figure in a dark hood appears at the window. The door is locked, but it doesn't matter. He grabs a piece of the gate that tumbled off the front of his car and uses it to smash the window. Glass falls down on me, and I scramble to the other side of the car. There's nowhere to go. Before I can grab hold of the door handle, he releases the lock on the door, opens it, and takes me by the ankles. Dragging me out of the seat causes glass to dig into my hands and scrape along the side of my face. His hand muffles any more screams that I hope will reach teenagers in the woods or people living nearby.

I fight and kick, but the position he has me in gravely limits my mobility. Tossing me into the backseat of his car, he holds me down with his thighs and binds my wrists with tape. A gag goes into my mouth, and he hobbles my legs before slamming the door closed.

The last thing I see is him reaching into the glove compartment and coming out with a syringe. The sharp pain in my arm comes an instant before blackness.

CHAPTER THIRTY-NINE

This comes only in flashes:

I don't know how long I'm in the back of the car. My eyes open for just a few moments, long enough to look up through the windows and see streetlights passing overhead.

The sky goes into the darkness of the middle of the night. The next time I open my eyes, it's a pale shade of gray. Then the sun stings in them. It's been many hours, and as far as I know, the car hasn't stopped. I can't move, and I realize the man who took me has tied me down to the seat.

When the car finally stops, I struggle to sit up, but can't. He comes to the door and opens it, reaching inside to release me and drag me out. Another man is standing just a few feet away. With closely cropped blonde hair and a pale blue shirt, he stares on with no expression on his face.

It's only when they've both taken hold of me and are dragging me across the parking area that I glanced back and realize we didn't arrive in the same car he stuffed me into in Virginia. At some point, he took my unconscious body out of the back seat and tied me into another car. It means the vehicle didn't stand out going down the highway, and the camera footage from the storage unit will be useless for tracing me.

I don't make it easy for them, but the men are stronger, and despite my struggling, they soon get me to the door of The Tower. Ruth is already sitting in the floral room when they bring me to her and drop me down onto the couch. She looks at me with barely a reaction.

"Gentlemen, don't you think you could do better for our guest? She is very special," she says.

The men release my feet and take the gag from my mouth.

"What the fuck is wrong with you people?" I demand the instant my mouth is free. "Let me go right now. I am a federal agent!"

It doesn't ruffle Ruth. She takes a sip of tea and settles the cup down onto a saucer.

"Would you like something? Priscilla makes the most incredible treats."

I feel like I'm looking at a hologram. She can't be real. None of this can be. Yet it is. This is what drew Everly in. These are the walls that brought her to the brink of death. I stand and start to move toward the door, but the two men take me by the shoulders and push me back. The hood has fallen away, and I meet eyes with my captor.

"Let. Me. Go," I growl.

A slight frown turns her lips down.

"I so hoped you would be happier about our invitation to welcome you into the Society."

"What?" I spit.

"Yes." Her smile returns. "I was so impressed by you during your first visit. The moment I saw you, I knew you were meant to be here, Sister Rebecca."

"No!" I shout at her. "I want nothing to do with you people! Do you have any idea the shit you're in for? Accosting a federal agent?"

Ruth leers at me with those impassive eyes but doesn't move a muscle. Just continues on like I haven't said anything.

"I know this might be hard for you to understand. It can be difficult to wrap your head around the truly awesome force surrounding you. But I promise you; you are worthy. You have been chosen. Lucas spoke of you that very night. He told me he had a vision of a new light coming into his life. A brighter light than he has ever seen. Sister Rebecca. A treasure to be cherished above all others."

"You're disgusting," I tell her.

Ruth rises to her feet.

"It takes time with some. The Existence holds strong to the most desirable and precious. But we will deliver you from it and purify you for the New Time. You don't have to be afraid. We're here to guide you."

I stand again, and she looks to the side.

"Jeremiah. Take her. This one will need you."

I lift my hands over my head and yank them down as hard as I can, pulling them apart at my waist. The movement causes the tape to snap, and I'm free to move. But there's nowhere to go. I get only one solid punch in before another needle sinks into my arm, and I collapse into waiting arms.

I don't know how much time has passed when I open my eyes again. I'm lying on a cold stone floor, and the only light comes from a lamp outside the doorway. The smell of death and rot invades my lungs. I can taste it. A dark silhouette forms in the doorway, and I pull myself up to face him.

"So, what's supposed to happen to me down here?" I ask.

"This is where you will start your purification."

"Is this what you did to her? Is this how you broke Everly?"

"She didn't need to be broken. She knew the gift being offered to her and happily accepted it."

"Until what? What happened that made it all change?"

"She lost her way. The Existence reached her soul, and she needed to be re-purified," he says flatly.

"Is that what you call stringing her up like a pig for slaughter? How long did it take you to find her, Ian?"

His head twitches slightly, as if the sound of the name is offensive.

"My name is Jeremiah."

"No. That's what they call you here. That's what they've brainwashed you into believing." I remember the research I was doing right before Sam arrived at my house with the pictures of the mass grave victims. "Your name is Ian Mills. You were declared missing six years ago from Vermont. How does it feel knowing your family is still looking for you?"

"They aren't my family. They are part of The Existence and aren't worthy to be in the New Time."

A bitter smile flickers on my lips.

"Where's Payton, Ian? Or have you not brought her here yet? That's why you married her, right? You knew she couldn't be compelled to testify against you if you were married."

Jeremiah – or Ian – stays quiet for a long moment. I know I'm right. I'll just need to keep him talking long enough for the Bureau to get here.

"How long will it be before she's branded, Ian? Oh, I'm sorry. Jeremiah. Whatever your name is. You know, I knew something was wrong when she talked about you getting married. It wasn't what a mother would do. At least, not one still in control of her mind. Then something she said stuck with me. Penelope wouldn't want her to be sad. She would want her to celebrate the future to come. Specifically chosen words, don't you think? Exactly the ones Ruth used to describe the event happening the day Everly died. The same event that brought her to her breaking point three years ago when you let them throw her away to be tortured for six months. I'll admit you chose a poetic date to kill her."

"She had to be sacrificed."

"Why? Because she had the guts to escape? Or because she made all of you look like fools by doing it?"

"She insulted Lucas and tainted the Society. Lucas had taken her as his and brought her into his Circle of Light. She belonged to him. She was a part of The Essence necessary to bring about the New Time. Leaving was an offense to the entire Society. A threat to our future.

They sent me for her. She was a wayward sheep, and I was meant to shepherd her back."

"They sent you to hunt her. They erased you out of their records and pretended you didn't exist, so no one could trace you to them. You weren't a shepherd; you were an assassin."

"I wanted to bring her back. The future was waiting for her. She could have had everything. Lucas favored her. She was special to him, and he wanted only what was best for her," Ian says.

"And that means being beaten and starved and raped for months?" I ask. "How is that what's best for her?"

"Everyone has to sacrifice for the coming time. We must purge ourselves of what holds us to The Existence so we can walk into the New Time," he says.

The way he's talking makes my skin crawl. I step closer to him.

"But you couldn't force her back. You couldn't break her again. Not like the first time."

"She thought she was safe being with Michael, untouchable. The Existence had too strong a hold on her. She was damaged and destroyed in the eyes of the Society and of Lucas. It devastated him, but as soon as she committed the unforgivable offense of marrying another man, he knew she was ruined. She had to be given up," he says.

"But by then, you were already using Payton to get close to her. You saw how vulnerable she was and latched onto her right after Everly met Michael. You injected yourself into her life, so she entwined herself with you. You gave her attention and validation, and she gave you access to Everly. I have to admit, making sure the doors were locked from the inside was smart. If you could make it look like a suicide, no one would look twice at you, and you could bring your new lamb to slaughter at Lucas's feet."

I let that echo in the room for a while, searching for something, anything, in his face. But it's all a show. I'm just trying to drag it out as long as I can. I have no idea how long has passed since I called Eric, but they can't be far away now.

"Daniel thought no one knew about the doors connecting the two houses. A little quirk of the design when Michael did renovations. They rarely ever used them. Even Daniel would walk out of his house and go around to the front door rather than go through that passage. But Payton knew about it. She was close with Daniel, and he probably shared it with her. Tell me, Ian. Did she know? Did she know you were going to kill Everly? Everly was brave, Ian. You never recognized that. You weren't expecting it. She never told Michael who you were."

"That wasn't bravery," Ian scoffs. "She knew what we were capable of. What the Society could do to Michael if he crossed us. He wasn't worthy. He was a waste of time and energy. You see, ours is so much more precious, more valuable, than that in the Existence. To hurt him out of spite would just be wasteful. But she knew we could eliminate him quickly and easily. She didn't tell him about me because she thought I would give up. She believed I would eventually get tired of her not complying and leave her alone to live her deceitful, heretic life. But that would never happen. She belonged to us.

"No, she didn't," I say. "She never did. You had her on borrowed time, but she was stronger than you could ever be. You might have killed her, but you couldn't take away who she was. The world will never forget who Everly was."

"Sister Abigail," he growls through his teeth.

"No. That wasn't her name. No one will ever say it again. Except you. Did you call her that when you talked to Payton about her? Did you slip and forget her real name? Or did you manage to keep it inside, so you didn't need to tell her what you were going to do?" I ask.

"She didn't need to know."

"But isn't she chosen for the future to come? Shouldn't she shed all that is around her and understand the sacrifices that need to be made?" I ask sarcastically. "What did you tell her? When you had to leave your honeymoon that morning, how did you explain it? You had the timing down well. Fast enough to get to Daniel's house, use Payton's key to get inside knowing full well his cameras only record when he sets them, which he doesn't do during the day, slip through the passage while he was in the shower, kill Everly, set up that whole scene, and then slip back out through Michael's office door so Daniel would never know you were there."

I let out an overly dramatic breath. "Wow. I'm tired just thinking about it. I'm guessing you caught up with her in the bathroom, just like Daniel did. That's why there's no sign of a struggle in the bedroom. And whatever drug you just used to cheat me out of our lovely road trip together... I know of several that are undetectable in standard toxicology reports. But I promise I'll make sure her body is properly tested."

"It's a nice puzzle you worked out for yourself, but you'll never be able to prove it," Ian says.

"Oh, but I can. At least, the prosecutors will be able to. You see, I know something you don't."

"What?" he asks, his voice arrogant.

"You aren't special, Ian. You think you're one of the favorites, destined for a place at Lucas's right hand and an eternity of pleasure. But you are disposable. They'll work the last drop of use out of you, then throw you away just like they do the others in your rank. Now that you've eliminated Everly for them, that time will likely be coming soon."

"You don't know what you're talking about," he says through gritted teeth.

"Don't I? What's on your wrist?"

He glances down at the inside of his left wrist.

"It's a tattoo, isn't it?" I scoff. "The Society didn't think twice about scrubbing you from their presence so no one could trace you back to them if you got caught. They told you to change the way you dressed, go back to your actual name, and leave your bracelet behind. But you just couldn't bear to not have that connection, the link to the only thing that gave you any validation. You had the symbol inside your bracelet tattooed to your wrist, just where it would be if you were still wearing it. Or if it was burned into you. It's incredible when you think about it. They have so much hold over you; you couldn't even see what you were doing. See, that's the thing. It's not the first time I've seen that symbol. I didn't realize it when I first came here. I didn't make the connection the first time I saw your tattoo. It was Daniel who reminded me. Everly wore a ring when she was here, and they would heat it up, so it burned her. They do the same to the men they're in the process of grinding down to a pulp. I investigated a case with eleven bodies found scattered around one area. All men. All beaten and starved. All with burns around their wrists. One had that symbol still clear on his skin. They're going to process you the same way, Ian. You're nothing to them. Just a tool."

He takes a step closer to me, his hands twitching at his sides, a mask of rage taking over his face.

"It's a compelling story. Too bad you won't have a chance to tell anyone."

CHAPTER FORTY

I have only a few seconds to decide exactly how to play this. I could rush him, but he would likely just slip back through the door and lock me in. I could try to taunt him and get him in further, but he could easily just decide that winning the argument would be leaving me here to rot. Or, I could go for the third option, slapping him hard across the face, and seeing if he decides to get violent.

This is another of those moments when my mind drifts to my gun. Not that it would have mattered even if I had it in the car with me. He would have taken it from me the second he tossed me in the backseat. This was going to take good old-fashioned thought and fight.

As Ian opens his mouth to speak, I open-hand slap him hard across his mouth, paint-brushing him backward a step.

The sting of his face on my palm is like being stung by hundreds of tiny ants, but it brings back all the adrenaline and training my body spent years honing into a fighting machine. I need to trust my training, going against every instinct I have, and let him lunge at me, maybe even let him connect with something before I fight back. It is vitally important for him to step further into the cell than closer to the door.

It works.

He flails out at me, fingers digging into my skin as he rips at my shirt, yanking me closer to him. His other hand balls into a fist and makes a long arc toward my face. I turn just in time for it to land on the side of my head instead, and I crumple to the ground, partially because of the force of the hit and partially to lull him further. He lords over me, his shoulders raised and wide, doing his best to intimidate me into submission.

I look up, tears welling in my eyes.

"Please," I half-whisper, and a smirk crosses his lips.

"Please, don't–" I begin, but don't finish.

Instead, I leap up, smashing my fist in his unprotected jaw, uppercutting him hard and sending him sprawling to the ground. I leap onto his chest and smash my fist in his face again, and he turns, trying to get onto his knees. I roll against the turn and wrap myself around his back, pulling my arms around his neck in a choke.

He gurgles and claws at my arms, but I have the hold locked in, and slowly his fighting subsides. A few seconds of no movement let me know he is out, and I release him, letting his head thud against the ground hard. He's still breathing, but out cold, and it gives me enough time to try to escape.

I stand up, taking a second to catch my breath. I poke my head out of the cell door and look down the hallway. It's empty. I break for it, going the direction I remember being brought, and slam the cell door behind me. I hear it click into place as I get a few steps away.

I dart up the steps two at a time for a floor and round a corner. I get up to an entrance but press myself against the wall, carefully scanning the hall before stepping through it. No one is there, but I don't trust it. The shadows are long and dark, and I could be being monitored on security cameras somewhere. I have to keep hidden as best as possible and move quickly.

I duck behind a couch, making my way across the room and to the door on the far side. I place my ear against it and hear a voice, faint in the distance, as if the person was walking away. There is no echo, which tells me this door leads to the outside. I wait until the voices have disappeared and open the door as carefully and quietly as I can.

The cool breeze of the evening rushes in, chilling the beads of sweat running down my back. I step out into the courtyard and try to orient myself. The door has led me to an area I briefly remember seeing when I was here earlier with Sam. It must be the back door of The Tower.

I slide behind some bushes against the building and breathe to calm myself. I need to stay focused and not let the adrenaline cause me to do anything stupid. I have to get help to me, rather than try to escape the compound.

I stay there for several long minutes. All I need to do is wait and stay out of sight. Eric and Creagan are coming to get me. Aren't they? Eric got all my information. What's taking them so long?

I duck down even lower when another pair of men pass by. My heart is hammering. Another minute passes, and then another. But I can't wait any longer. For all I know, it could still be hours before they show up, and I don't have that kind of time. I have to find some way out of here. Now.

An idea pops into my head, and I run for the row of cars parked behind The Tower. My hands slam onto the drivers' side window of the nearest car. A sleek, brand new model. Exactly what I'm looking for. No keyhole for the ignition, which means it's activated by key fob. A car like this has got to be equipped with a variety of safety measures. My eyes slide over the dash and to the mirror. It has a button on it, large and white. An emergency button. One connected to GPS and EMS. Perfect.

I turn and look around frantically for something I can smash the window with. Anything that could break through the glass will do. There are no large rocks or poles or anything lying around, so I scope out a little farther. Finally, the moon shifts, giving me more visibility, illuminating my way ahead. And then I see it. There might not be an angel chorus along with it, but I'll take it.

On the side of The Tower, just yards from the parking lot is a gardener's shed. And it is open.

I run to it and grab a sledgehammer hanging on the wall. I snatch it from its place, heave it onto my shoulder, and run back to the car. I look around one last time, making sure the area is empty and noting where I will hide once I get this done, and then I hoist the hammer into the air.

"You smash mine. I'll smash yours," I mutter.

With a hard swing, I crash through the window, sending a loud wail of a siren into the air. I scramble into the car, slamming my hand on the button. A pleasant voice announces itself and asks what my emergency is.

"This is FBI agent Emma Griffin," I tell her as quickly and clearly as I can and rattle off my badge number. "Requesting immediate assistance at this location, repeat, immediate assistance, I am on the scene of multiple homicides and in imminent danger."

Before the voice on the other end can answer me, I run to my hiding spot, diving beneath some bushes on the building next to The Tower. I can still hear the faint sound of the emergency responder asking for me through the car speakers, but I can't call out to answer now. I just hope she'll pass along the message.

I nestle further into the shadows, peering out directly at The Tower. With a slow creak, the back door opens. I brace myself, holding a deep breath.

But I let it out. It isn't Ian or any of the men. It's the frail form of a woman. She stumbles out and tries to run, but her feet tangle under her, and she hits the ground. I rush out of my hiding spot and scoop my arms under hers, pulling her up as best I can so I can drag her with me to the hiding spot.

"Please," she whispers. "Please, help me. Please."

"I'm here," I tell her. "I've got you."

"Take me with you."

Her voice has nothing behind it, like the words are made up of breath and thought. Her eyes flutter closed, and her body sags against me.

"I have you. But you have to stay awake. Come on. Stay with me. We can't stay right here. We have to move toward the gate."

She nods weakly and manages to get to her feet. With me supporting her, she moves with me toward the shed. We get behind it just as I hear men shouting from The Tower. Ruth's voice rises above it.

"Find her. I want her brought to me."

The woman starts to sob, and I hold her closer, trying to quiet her.

"It's going to be fine. We just need to keep moving. Come on. Tell me where to go next. You know this place," I say.

"The fountain," she finally manages.

I look around the other side of the shed. A short distance away, I see a fountain; its water turned off for the night.

"Okay. When I tell you, you need to run as fast as you can. I'm here to help you. Alright?"

She nods.

"Everything is going to be okay," I tell her again. I really hope it will be.

I see the men now. They rush for the car I smashed, gathering around it and shouting at each other. We need to take advantage of their distraction. "Now."

I run and drag the girl with me to the fountain. It casts a dark shadow on the ground, and we hunker down into it. We're closer to the gate now, but not as close as I want to be. The girl is fading again. Her head lolls to the side, and she lets out a groan. All I can imagine is Everly and the strength it took to get out of here.

"Talk to me," I whisper. "Stay with me. Talk to me. What's your name?"

"Eloise," she murmurs.

"Is that your name? Or is that what they call you? I want to know your name. Your real name."

"Devon."

Her lips twitch as she says it, like she has to remember how, but it feels good.

"Devon. Hi, Devon. I'm Emma. How long has it been since someone has said your name?"

"Five years."

"Well, Devon, I will say it as many times as you need me to. We need to move again. Okay, Devon? We're going to head for that group of trees. I'm going to get you out of here. I promise, Devon. Now let's go!"

She nods, and we take off for the trees. Every time we run, we're in the open. I brace myself for the sound of heavy footfalls or the men shouting.

But that's not what I hear.

First, there is a gunshot. The bullet whizzes just past us into the night. They see us. My blood goes cold.

I hold Devon under my arm and duck, trying to find cover. But it's no use. There are too many of them, and I have nothing to hide behind.

I rest Devon to the ground and stand, prepared to face them, and protect her as much as I can. An instant later, the air around me splits.

Sirens. Blue lights washing over me.

My knees give way, and I sink down beside her.

The rest is a blur.

Booming voices over a megaphone. Officers scrambling over the wall. A car smashing into the gate. Arms scooping me up.

"Agent Griffin?" a voice asks. "Are you hurt? Do you need medical attention?"

"I'm fine," I insist. I'm tired and woozy and overwhelmed, but I'm not seriously hurt.

"Thanks for your tip. Great thinking out there. We were able to triangulate your location from the car."

My heart sinks.

"I, um," I try, but my words are slurred. Maybe Ian hit me harder than I thought. "Do you... I was working with Sherriff Sam Johnson in Sherwood, Virginia..."

"He's fine. A bit battered up, but he's going to pull through. He's in the hospital in Virginia. He told me to tell you Eric is on his way."

I nod, suddenly exhausted. With the help of another agent, I stagger my way to the ambulance, Devon passed out on my shoulder, but am only dimly aware of handing her off to the EMT before I slump off into unconsciousness.

———

Two days later, I make my way down the hall into another hospital room. The doctors insist on keeping me for another couple of days even though I know I'm fine to go home. I just got punched in the face once and had some minor cuts and bruises. But I can move around, and that means I have a visit to make.

This time when I walk into the room, she's partially sitting up. Her hair is clean and brushed, spread out on the pillow around her, and the IV in her arm has brought some color to her cheeks.

"Hi, Devon," I smile. "It's good to see you awake."

"How can I thank you?" she asks, her voice still soft. "You saved my life."

I shake my head. "You don't need to. But there's something I want to show you." I take out my phone and bring it to the side of the bed. Sitting on one of the chairs, I lean close and hold the picture up to her. Devon's eyes well with tears as she runs her fingertips across it. "She's the one you should thank. Her name is Everly Zara."

EPILOGUE

"I asked you that earlier!"

"You did not ask me that earlier."

"Yes, I did! And you said you couldn't disprove me."

"Nope."

"I suspected Mrs. White in the ballroom with the revolver. And you said you couldn't prove me wrong," I insist.

"You started to suspect Mrs. White, then you changed your mind and suspected Miss Peacock instead," Sam tells me.

"Which I really didn't appreciate because I was on my way to the lounge," Janet pipes up.

I look down at my clue sheet in front of me.

"Well, shit."

Everybody laughs, and I toss the paper and pen onto the board.

"It's alright, babe. You'll solve a murder one of these days," Sam winks, leaning over to kiss my cheek.

"Mr. Boddy just needs to stop getting his ass killed. That's a solution." My phone rings, where I left it on the counter across the room, and I stand up to get it. "Let this be my official nomination for Twister next week."

"I'll start stretching now," Paul says.

I laugh and reach up to loosen my pendant from where it's gotten tangled in my hair. I don't remember wearing this necklace with my mother, but every time I put it on, I can feel her closer. I pick up my phone and send a smile over my shoulder to Sam.

"Hello?" I say.

"Emma?"

"Yes?"

The call ends, and I look down at the screen. "That was weird."

"Who was it?" Sam asks.

My phone alerts to a new message coming in, and I open it.

"Listen carefully," I read.

"To what?" Sam asks, coming across the room to me. We turn away from Paul and Janet. They're wonderful to have as friends and all, but I don't exactly want to involve them in this whole tangled mess that is my last few months.

"There's a video."

I open it and immediately recognize the Richmond bus station. A face appears in front of the camera.

"That's one of the victims of the bombing," Sam says. "Mary. She was a vlogger."

The pretty young girl grins at the camera she holds high above her and scans back and forth to show more of her surroundings. She's saying something about picking up luggage tags at the desk. The camera swoops to the side and suddenly catches the man in front of her.

"That's Greg," I say, jumping slightly.

He leans toward the man behind the desk and says something, but I don't understand him.

"Listen carefully," Sam reminds me, pointing at the screen.

I scan back several seconds, turn up the volume, and try to drown out Mary's voice. When I see Greg lean toward the man, I zoom in and notice he's handing him something. Then he speaks.

"Give this to Emma Griffin."

The End

Dear Reader,

Thank you for your continued support. I really appreciate that you read the third book in my series!
I hope you liked this book just as much as The Girl That Vanished.
If you can please leave me a review for this book as well, I would appreciate that enormously.
Your reviews allow me to get the validation I need to keep going as an indie author.
Just a moment of your time is all that is needed.

Again, thank you for reading The Girl In The Manor.
I promise to always do my best to bring you thrilling adventures.

Yours,
A.J. Rivers

P.S. The Girl Next Door is your next adventure in the Emma Griffin FBI Mysteries.

P.S.S. If for some reason you didn't like this book or found typos or other errors, please let me know personally. I do my best to read and respond to every email at aj@riversthrillers.com

STAYING IN TOUCH WITH A.J.

Type the link below in your internet browser now to join my mailing list and get your free copy of Edge Of The Woods.

https://dl.bookfunnel.com/ze03jzd3e4

MORE EMMA GRIFFIN FBI MYSTERIES

Emma Griffin's FBI Mysteries is the new addictive best-selling series by A.J. Rivers. Make sure to get them all below!

Visit my author page on Amazon to order your missing copies now! Now available in paperback!

ALSO BY A.J. RIVERS